# THE PAINTED LOBSTER MURDERS

COZY CRAFT

BOOK 2

MILLIE RAVENSWORTH

# 1

The problems started with the arrival of a dog at the birthday party.

A chunky and handsome corgi with a collar but no lead came bounding into the shop on the heels of birthday boy Monty Starling and his mother, Caroline, who was footing the bill for the event.

"Oh, a corgi!" said Penny. What she really wanted to say was, "Oh a dog in our sewing shop, please put it on a lead and keep it well away from our stock," but Caroline Starling was paying the bill and she didn't want to get too stern with a customer.

Penny had been managing the Cozy Craft sewing shop for a little over three months at the request of her Nanna Lem, who was still recovering from a foot injury. The shop felt a little like an elderly boat at sea, and not just because its floors were made of ancient creaking wood. Penny was trying to steer it a course through the choppy waters of modern commerce and, although it probably wasn't sinking as rapidly as it had been when she'd first turned up, it was still taking on water here and there. The need to keep things on an even keel while not rocking the boat was very much at the front of her mind, alongside countless other nautical metaphors.

Nanna Lem had run the shop for decades, and the mountains of stock that swamped nearly every room on its upper floors were testament to that grand history. When Penny had come down from London earlier in the year to help run the place, she had been alarmed to discover it had devolved into little more than a joke shop, selling cheap and unpleasant fancy dress outfits and a paltry selection of haberdashery items to the most loyal of customers.

Today's birthday party was part of Penny's attempts to rejuvenate the business. The recently redecorated workshop upstairs was ready for the guests. Downstairs in the shop itself, a dozen rickety but serviceable seats had been set up for returning parents to sit on during the fashion show that would be the party's climax.

Hosting children's birthday parties was uncharted waters for the shop and Penny wanted it to go well. There would be sewing and the awarding of prizes, and there was a cake for the birthday boy. The cake was a huge tray bake sent over from Wallerton's cake shop in the market place. It was more than a metre wide, and covered with green and white gooey frosting to represent a football field. Penny was of the opinion that no boy, no matter how many friends he had, could want a cake that big. But, again, Penny was not about to disagree with a paying customer.

Leaving Caroline and her bouncing dog to go about their business for a couple of hours, Penny took Monty up the narrow stairs to the workshop room, already full of noisy and rumbunctious ten-year-old boys. Monty's arrival only served to increase both the volume and the rambunctiousness.

"Can I please have your attention, everyone?" Izzy yelled.

Izzy, Penny's cousin, co-operator of the shop, dressmaker extraordinaire and undaunted dreamer, had no issues with shouting at children.

The noise dropped a little and the boys were assigned to groups. Every instruction, it seemed, needed to be shouted and repeated a number of times. The plan for the party was to make camouflage utility vests, sleeveless jackets which were easy to construct and onto which they could add pockets and all sorts of extras if they wanted.

"Make your choice of fabric and thread and then we can talk about embellishments. Got that?" shouted Izzy.

"Miss! How will we each be able to sew? There aren't enough machines!" came a voice.

"There will be a machine and a workstation for each group of two," said Izzy.

As construction commenced, Penny and Izzy spent much of their time making sure that metal hardware and fingers were kept clear of the sewing machine needles, as nearly all of the boys would insist on stomping their feet on the pedals to make the machines sew as fast as they possibly could.

Soon, all of the boys had finished sewing their utility vests, and it was time to use the pliers to add fasteners. As predicted, this was a big hit, and some of the vests had many more fasteners than were strictly necessary. Izzy showed them how to add eyelets as well.

Penny and Izzy exchanged glances.

"I think this has gone well," said Penny. "Time to set up for the show?"

Penny went to the kitchenette, took three bottles of Co-op prosecco (for the parents) and two bottles of cola (for the children) out of the fridge, and carried them downstairs. As she entered the shop, she heard a noise, a burbling whimper, but she couldn't immediately place it. Frowning, she followed the sound to the front of the shop.

"Oh no!"

The dog was still in her shop. The handsome brown and white corgi with bright eyes and large curved ears was *still* in her shop.

Except it wasn't entirely brown and white now. It had a dribbling green goatee beard. Somehow — somehow! For the cake had *definitely* been on the counter and the corgi was so *small*! — somehow, the blasted dog had dragged the protective lid from the birthday cake, bringing more than half of the semi-solid frosting with it onto the floor. Most of the green football field had been stripped back to reveal the brown cake beneath, becoming less a professional pitch and more a muddy quagmire in the process.

The corgi looked up at Penny, seemingly very pleased with itself.

Stunned though she was, Penny could see that, quite obviously, this wasn't her problem. Caroline Starling had paid for the cake and Caroline Starling had left her dog in the shop. She would just notify the woman and, although she would express sympathy and propose whatever helpful solutions came to mind, the blame would pass over to the boy's mum.

She texted Caroline.

YOU LEFT YOUR DOG BEHIND. IT'S HERE IN THE SHOP.

The reply came almost instantly.

I DON'T HAVE A DOG.

Penny's stomach lurched. "Oh no. Oh no, no, no!"

Not her dog? Not *her* dog?!

# 2

At that moment, there came a tap on the door. Penny, in her heightened state of distress, jumped. It was Aubrey Jones — painter and decorator, a great help in refurbishing the tired old dress shop, a friendly face in this sometimes insular market town and, despite what Izzy kept insinuating, not Penny's boyfriend in any shape or form. Aubrey had agreed to come over and help judge the boys' final designs in a fashion show, in the guise of an entirely fictitious fashion celebrity. Penny expected Izzy to point to this helpfulness as evidence of the boyfriend-girlfriend relationship that did not exist at all between the young man and Penny. Penny would tell Izzy to shut up if she did.

Penny let Aubrey in, attempting to form words to express her distress at the whole dog-cake situation, but failing. She fell back on pointing at the dog and the cake and the upstairs and making small mewling sounds.

"Ohh, this is tricky," said Aubrey.

That was an understatement.

"Yes, I see that this is tricky. We can fix things though," he continued, his hands on Penny's shoulders. "Deep breaths. Whose dog is this?"

Penny shrugged to indicate that she had no idea. "Sorry. It came in with the boy's mother. I thought it had gone out with her again. Look what it's done!"

Aubrey nodded. "When will the grown-ups be here?"

Penny checked her watch. "Ten minutes for the early birds."

"Izzy's got the kids upstairs?"

Penny nodded.

Aubrey thought for a moment. "I'll go and meet the kids, make sure they're all set for the show. Izzy can come down here and do something with the cake. You sort out the dog and then make sure you're ready to greet the parents."

"Sort out the dog, sort out the dog." Penny stared at its grinning face as it licked frosting from around its mouth. She gave a low whistle and to her surprise it bounded over. "Hello there!" she said, with less enthusiasm than she felt. "Do you have a name?" The dog had a collar, but there was nothing engraved on it.

"He'll probably want a drink," said Aubrey, from halfway up the stairs.

"He?"

"Yes, definitely a he," replied Aubrey with a nod towards the creature.

Penny fetched a bowl of water and the dog slurped

greedily. She found an offcut of tana lawn fabric and used it to wipe his face free of cake frosting.

Izzy clattered down the stairs. “Oh my, Penny! How bad is it?”

“Bad!”

Izzy went over to the cake and peered in the box. “I think I can remodel what’s there so that it looks more or less as it should. This perspex ruler should work wonders on cake frosting.”

“But we can’t let people eat a cake that a dog has licked! No offense,” she said to the dog.

“If we cut it up at the earliest opportunity we can make sure to remove the frosting from the top. It’ll be fine, Penny. But I think that dog needs to go out.”

Penny found a length of cotton tape and formed a makeshift lead for the dog, and then she took it for a walk around Market Hill.

Up until Nanna Lem’s request for her to come and help scatterbrained Izzy run the shop, Penny had not been in Framlingham for years. The change of pace she had experienced moving from London to Fram had been immense. If London was a city that never slept then Framlingham was a town that was happy to spend several days a week mooching about in its dressing gown and slippers before going back to bed. And Penny loved the rural market town for it. It was a place where people could take the time to get to know each other, where family time and social events were not hurriedly brushed aside in the day’s hectic schedule. Among the leaning stone buildings and wibbly back alleys, Penny had found a town where she could unwind and... breathe.

Even now, with a hundred things to worry about, it was pleasantly diverting to pick out a route around the ancient marketplace and see the world through the eyes of a dog. The simple joy of examining every corner and wagging a tail at every passer-by was infectious. Old McGillicuddy and Timmy sat in their usual spot near the centre of the marketplace. The old man waved and Penny briefly wandered over so the two dogs could have sniff of each other.

When Penny returned to the shop a few minutes later she had a smile on her face.

"I've found a box he can have a sleep in," Izzy called to her. "Behind the counter."

Penny showed the dog to the box and was relieved that when, after a brief inspection, he circled for a few moments and then lay down in it.

"What do you think of the cake?" asked Izzy.

Penny examined the patch-up job and had to concede that it looked reasonable. If the bakers were to see it, they would, no doubt, be appalled at the destruction of their work, but by most people's standards it was good enough. The frosting had been smeared out to a thinner depth but the football pitch was green again.

"Let's put it as far away as we can from the audience," suggested Izzy.

Parents had started to arrive, and Penny took care to sit them all down ready for the show.

Izzy and Penny exchanged a smile as the last of the parents were handed their glasses of fizz and took their seats.

Caroline Starling, drink in hand, dashed Penny's optimism in an instant by saying, "And where is the cake?"

She had begun to pick her way through the chairs, with a couple of other guests in her wake, all eager to view the baked creation. Penny couldn't think of a way to stop them, and worse still, they all had phones in their hands, ready to take pictures that would surely broadcast the shop's carelessness and their hasty reconstruction far and wide.

"Why is my audience not ready for the show?" demanded Aubrey. "I was told that everything was in place! It is time for the fashion show!"

The voice that boomed down the stairs was Aubrey's, but it was not Aubrey's quiet demeanour. It had the rich fruitiness and the unplaceable accent of a continental extrovert.

As Izzy flapped surprised parents back to their seats, Aubrey and the boys descended to begin their fashion show.

Boys paraded, parents clapped, prizes were awarded and, in a blink-and-you'll-miss-it manoeuvre, a cake was whisked out, candles extinguished and the cake hurried away again to be cut up for guests.

"Aubrey properly saved our bacon," Penny whispered to Izzy.

It was undoubtedly true. If Izzy was right about Aubrey being ideal boyfriend material — and Penny wasn't admitting he was! — then perhaps she ought to ask him out, perhaps even just for a thank you drink for helping cover up today's disasters.

# 3

As the boys departed, Penny handed out party gift bags.

"What's that you're putting in them?" asked Izzy, eyeing the bulging bags.

"Last of the costume stuff," said Penny. "I realised that there were enough of these celebrity masks for them all to have one each."

Izzy turned to watch the last of the guests making their way out of the shop. "Aw, even the Brad Pitt mask. I used to say hello to him every morning."

Penny frowned at the departing boy. "I thought that was a Donald Trump mask."

"No, it says Brad Pitt on the package."

"Blimey. I'm glad we're giving them away. Anyway, it's a celebration of sorts, I think. Would you say we've properly arrived as a sewing shop now? The workshop went really well."

A slender, silver-haired woman was the last to leave. "I have to congratulate you on a job well done," she said.

"Oh, thank you."

She extended a hand. Izzy shook it.

"Fliss Starling," said the woman. "Grandmother to the birthday boy. They do spoil him, don't they?"

"I couldn't possibly say," replied Penny, diplomatically.

"I could," added Izzy, less so.

"The boy is named after a dear departed friend," said Fliss. "I wonder if you could perhaps help me with a small problem that I have."

Penny smiled. "Why don't you try us?"

"Do you make garments? One-off commissions?" she asked.

Penny managed to flash a swift look at Izzy, who was in the habit of underselling their services. "We can do that, but they can be expensive, depending on what it is."

"Never mind that," snapped Fliss. "It's something of a unique emergency. I was planning to engage Wickham Dress Agency but my good friend Carmella is being a perfect pain in the rear at present, and perhaps you can help instead. You know about the upcoming Motor Show?"

"Um," Penny tried to remember something she had seen in the free local paper.

"Vintage cars from all of the classic eras, displayed in the heart of the town for a glorious weekend of motormania," said Izzy promptly. It made sense that Izzy would know all the details; she had probably written the article.

"Indeed. Well, my husband, Wills, owns one of the key

display pieces. You will appreciate of course that period dress is an important part of the aesthetic?"

"Oh, I can see that, yes!" said Penny. "Which classic era is your husband's car from?"

"It's a Derby Bentley from the thirties. He's only recently got it going properly."

"Lovely!" Penny had absolutely no idea what a Derby Bentley was or whether Derby was the model or where it came from but her mind was already swimming with vague images of round headlights, teeny doors and perhaps stylish running boards. She tried to picture clothes from the thirties, but came up lacking. What came after twenties flapper dresses but before wartime restrictions? What did they wear?

"Well, I had the most divine outfit, made from white linen. Beach pyjamas, they were delightful."

Penny didn't know which part to query first. Was it the concept of beach pyjamas or the fact that Fliss was referring to them in the past tense. "Did something happen?"

Fliss put a hand to her head. "I can hardly bear to talk about it. Wills had been doing maintenance. Filthy oil on his hands. Sometimes he forgets himself when I walked past... anyway, he caught me unawares. Black handprints on both buttcheeks. Can you imagine?"

Penny somehow found it far easier to imagine oily handprints on white linen than beach pyjamas in general.

"It's unsalvageable," continued Fliss, "and the motor weekend starts on Friday. We've got a house full of guests and I wouldn't normally ask but I saw this place and remembered that my dear friend, Gertie Masters, spoke highly of it. That's Gertie, the wife of our friend, Derek. Before she died, obviously.",

"Did she?" said Izzy.

Fliss glanced at the slender silver watch on her wrist. "I must be off. We've got four guests staying over at Saxtead Grange all week and certain people are not happy unless given their four-hourly feeds. But do say you can come over to inspect the damage and see if you can whizz something up in time."

"What time do you want us?" said Penny.

Fliss shrugged lightly. "G and T o'clock?"

"Four?" Penny hazarded.

Fliss laughed merrily, and Penny had no idea if she'd said something foolish.

"Yes! Four, it is," said Fliss. "I'll show you the one Wills ruined and then you can tell me if it's possible and what it will cost. Money is no object, mind! That car nut ruined it so he's paying. Saxtead Grange. If you get to the windmill, you've gone too far."

With that and no further information, she swept out. Penny half-expected her exit to be accompanied by the click of heels but Fliss wore white tennis shoes and bounced lightly for a woman her age.

Penny looked to Izzy. Izzy's eyes sparkled and she wore an expression of dreamy excitement.

"Can we do it?" asked Penny.

"Never say never," said Izzy.

Penny rotated her cousin by the shoulders so they were facing one another.

"Actually, in my experience, never is a very useful word.

People who never say never end up making waistcoats for pigs and selling poor quality Brad Pitt masks."

"We sell poor quality John Travolta masks too."

"Point is, can we do this and what will we charge?"

"It's the challenge that counts."

"Actually, it's being able to pay the bills and our wages that counts. That woman said money is no object."

"Are we going to fleece her just because she's rich?"

"No," said Penny firmly. "We are going to act like businesswomen and that means we're professional and value our time appropriately."

"Gotcha," said Izzy. Penny suspected she hadn't been listening to a word.

# 4

Izzy had paid full attention to what Penny had said, and came down into the shop dressed appropriately.

"What –" began Penny, "and I say this with all the love in my heart – what on earth are you wearing?"

Izzy had put on a crisp white shirt over her tartan trousers, and matched it with a bold red kipper tie. "A tie says business, fun but formal, yes?" suggested Izzy.

"Um, no. Please take it off," Penny asked.

Izzy did as she was told. It wasn't that Penny was in charge or anything; Izzy was firm on that point. Penny was like the signs at theme parks saying you had to be 'this' tall to ride, or maybe she was more like the high-speed terms and conditions bit at the end of adverts. Penny was an essential part of the world, not always a barrier to fun, but a necessary element of the whole experience.

"The dog liked it," said Izzy as she rolled the tie around her hand.

The corgi in the box by the counter looked up and whined. He seemed to have spent most of the afternoon snoozing, possibly sleeping off an unwise feast of green and white fondant icing.

"And we have to find his owner!" Penny called after her.

It was a forty minute walk from the town centre to Saxtead Grange. Both of them had driving licences but Penny had never needed a car in London and Izzy preferred to cycle everywhere, on a bicycle that seemed to be held together by colourful yarn.

The road out towards Saxtead was narrow, with an even narrower pavement. It was July, nearing the height of summer. The sun was bright and made golden splashes of light on the hawthorn bushes where birds played. The side road to the grange was winding and took them even further from other signs of civilisation until they came to the grange itself, alone in a sea of fields that stretched in all directions.

"Would you look at that," said Penny in awe.

Saxtead Grange was a massive old manor house, at least four hundred years old, she'd have guessed. Much of it was in the Tudor style with exposed beams of oak running between its plaster walls. Attached to it were two-storey wood-sided outbuildings, together forming a large horseshoe around a gravel courtyard. Red tiles, pink-painted plaster and black-painted wood, all in the Suffolk style. In front of it was an expansive manicured garden.

"They've got their own fishing lake," said Izzy, pointing at the rectangular pool outside the front of the house.

"It's just a fish pond," said Penny, although its size had her doubting her own words.

"We can definitely charge this woman what we want," said Izzy.

They crunched up the driveway.

"You know that thing where poor peasants feel over-awed and intimidated by the trappings of their social betters?" Izzy whispered.

"We're not peasants and they're not our social betters," Penny told her.

"Yeah, but I'm feeling it anyway."

"Me too," Penny conceded.

From somewhere in the courtyard area, a man's voice was angrily shouting, "Blast it! Monty! Monty! Come here!"

There was the sound of a familiar voice chiding the man, and then Fliss Starling appeared around the corner. She had changed from earlier and was wearing a light floral summer dress with a translucent throw gathered over her exposed shoulders.

"Apologies for Derek there. The man has only one volume setting. Ah, how lovely that my dressmaking saviours are here!"

"Right you are, Ma'am," said Izzy, and performed a little curtsey.

"I hope we can be of some assistance," added Penny.

"Drinks on the lawn. Best to stay out of the house and away from Carmella for the time being."

Iron chairs and table were set out on the neatly trimmed grass a short distance from the circular brick wall of an old fashioned well. There was a silver trolley of glasses and bottles. A middle-aged woman in a simple black suit brought out a jug of orange-pink loveliness with mint and cucumber floating in it.

"Thank you, Susan," said Fliss as the woman set it down. "I had Susan make up a jug of Pimm's even though I don't usually until Wimbledon season. God knows, I need a drink right now." She poured herself a big sloshing glass full of ice. "Drink?"

Izzy looked up from inspecting the deep dark well. Penny nodded with polite agreeability. She didn't want to drink too much. There was a two mile walk home to contemplate.

"Tell me about beach pyjamas," she said as she stirred mint leaves around her glass with a straw. "They sound lovely."

Fliss gave a small smile. "They used the word pyjamas to describe loungewear back then, so beach pyjamas were really a casual sun suit with wide legs. Gorgeous designs, too. I have no idea why we don't all still wear them."

"We've got some lovely white linen at the shop," said Izzy. "And I think I saw a pattern recently that might just tickle your fancy."

Fliss pulled a cynical expression, as if doubting that her fancy could be so easily tickled.

Izzy tapped on her phone and pulled up an image. "Here, Ma'am. Wide leg overalls. It's a reproduction of a thirties pattern."

Fliss took the phone, her face still doubtful, but then she saw the picture and gasped. "Oh my! It's a one-piece, but such adorable detail! It would fit the theme so perfectly. And because it has the look of a set of overalls it hints at the idea that I am the mechanic for the car, what a hoot!"

The man's shouting came again, this time from somewhere on the other side of the building. "Monty! Monty!" The cry was greeted by a woman's indecipherable shout from an upper window.

"Although sometimes I do rather wish they'd all take their cars and buzz off somewhere else," muttered Fliss, taking a hurried and greedy slurp of her cocktail. "House guests for the weekend," she explained. "Four of them joining me and Wills, my husband. You heard Derek Masters back there. God knows how Jacqui puts up with it all, listening to that man shout her husband's name all the time. I know I struggle. And then of course there's our friends the Mountjoys, up from Wickham Market. Frank and Carmella. You know them?"

"Can't say we do," said Penny.

"He breeds pigs. She breeds contempt. And owns the Wickham Dress Agency."

It sounded like Fliss had a confusing roster of guests staying at her place. It was no wonder she needed Susan the housemaid or whatever the woman's job title was.

"Anyway, Ma'am," said Izzy, trying to press on. "It's a great design. The pattern is made in the States, but we can buy it as a download and get it printed locally."

Fliss, despite distractions, was entranced. "I'd love a quote for getting this made up. What is the linen like?"

"I have a sample here," said Izzy, and brought out a large swatch of pale linen. It was soft and smooth but had the heft which gave linen its reassuringly durable feel.

"That is delightful," said Fliss, and then gasped as if an

idea had suddenly come to her, although Penny suspected that whatever she was about to say had been in her mind all along. "I know what would take this design from adorable to absolutely iconic. I don't know if you could pull it off, but I've had the most wonderful idea."

"What is it?"

"The Schiaparelli lobster dress."

"Sorry, Ma'am?" asked Izzy.

"Let me find a picture to show you what I mean. Bear with." She propelled herself from her seat and hurried to the house.

Penny leaned over to Izzy. "Why do you keep calling her 'Ma'am'?" she whispered.

"Was I?"

"You were. And you curtseyed."

Izzy pulled a face. "I think my social class reflexes have kicked in. My body's gone all Downton Abbey. I can't stop it."

"Well, try!" Penny hissed.

"They've got servants!" Izzy hissed back, shielding her hand with the other as she pointed at the house.

"Just cos a woman brings out drinks, doesn't mean she's a servant."

"No one brings us drinks," Izzy countered.

Penny sipped her cocktail. It was fruity and filled with warm spices and a powerful quantity of alcohol. It was, she had to admit, delicious, and she could imagine herself drinking and enjoying it in vast quantities.

"Here!" called Fliss as she scuttled back across the lawn, a heavy fashion book in her hands.

Penny and Izzy leaned in as Fliss sat down and saw an image of a white dress with an orange waistband and a large orange mark on the skirt.

"That is a lobster on the dress," Penny said.

"Yes, see?" said Fliss. "In the thirties this was one of the most famous dresses in the world. It was designed by Elsa Schiaparelli and the lobster was painted by Dali."

"Dali? Melting clocks and weird paintings Dali?" asked Izzy.

"Yes. The Spanish artist and Schiaparelli were friends. He painted this lobster on the dress. The dress was owned by Wallis Simpson."

For a half second Penny wondered if Wallis Simpson was yet another one of the house guests at Saxtead Grange, and then she recalled her history.

"The same Wallis Simpson that prompted the King of England to abdicate?" she asked.

"Yes, that exact same one. Although I don't think the dress played any part in that. I was thinking that it would be fun to have a lobster on these overalls. Do you see what I'm thinking? It would be a sort of homage. And it serves as a bold expression of the woman's feminine power."

"Do lobsters symbolise feminine power?" asked Penny.

"Dali had some interesting opinions on the matter," said Fliss.

The phone was beside the image in the book. Penny looked at the generous flared trousers of the overalls and the skirt of the lobster dress.

"You're right," said Izzy. "It could look amazing."

"Yes, but can you do it?" asked Fliss. "The sewing and the painting?"

"Of course we can."

"Can we?" said Penny.

"Of course! Never say never!"

Penny held her tongue and decided to say nothing.

"Hello, girls!" called a white-haired man in a blue newsboy cap, crossing the lawn to them. "How's the fashion plans coming on?"

"Penny, Izzy, this is the bane of my life and cause of my current predicament, my husband, Will." Despite the words, she said it with obvious fondness.

The man tilted his head and gave an easy and somewhat raffish grin. "Ah, me and my thoughtless grease monkey hands. Bad Willy, naughty Willy." He slapped himself playfully on the wrist and laughed at his own joke. "I hope you girls can help me make amends. Has she explained that money is no object?"

"It might have been mentioned," said Penny diplomatically.

"Anything to soothe my sugarplum."

The shouting began again in the house, the man's cries of "Monty!" and the woman shouting back at him.

"You could soothe my nerves by shutting those two up," said Fliss. "Strangle the lot of them if you will."

"Seems old Derek has lost his dog," said Wills.

"I thought you said he was calling for Jacqui's husband," said Penny.

"Isn't Monty your grandson's name?" said Izzy.

"Dog named after the dear departed husband," said Fliss. "Grandson too. Only gets confusing near dinner times."

"Dog?" said Penny.

"Yes. A little corgi. Adorable. Unlike his owner."

Penny and Izzy looked at each other.

# 5

Derek Masters, owner of Monty the dog (as opposed to Monty the grandson) was by the garages in the courtyard. The garages had been barns in centuries past but now, with black doors thrown wide, had been transformed into a storage and workshop space. Three old cars were lined up, one red, one green, one cream.

Izzy understood the joy that an object of beauty could bring and, even though she had very little understanding of cars, the curved lines and hand-finished fittings spoke to her of beautiful design and craftsmanship.

"This one is my pride and joy," said Derek, running a cloth over the hinged bonnet of the open top car. It was the deep red of ripe plums. "Nineteen thirty-six MG Midget. Wills and Frank might have bigger beasts but it's what you do with it that counts, eh?" The balding, bewhiskered man eyed

Penny and Izzy, his complexion not dissimilar to that of his car. "Now, which of you two has snaffled my dog?"

"We haven't snaffled any dog," said Izzy.

"He just wandered into our shop in town," added Penny. "And then ate a cake."

"What cake?" asked Derek, with apparent concern, and Fliss's eyes widened in sudden suspicion.

"No cake," said Izzy quickly. "No cake at all."

Derek whirled on Will and waggled a long-handled socket spanner at him. "This is your fault for not having secure fences."

"Derek, dear, we don't have dogs that need secure fences," said Fliss. "You're only here for the week. You *are* only here for the week, aren't you?" She raised a hand and then seemed to realise there was a cocktail in it.

"Well, I'll have that dog back now if it's all the same to you," Derek said.

"You are absolutely welcome to come and collect it," said Penny.

Derek tapped his car. "Girl needs a run out, but she's only a two-seater."

"We walked here," said Izzy.

"Which of you two..." His gazed flicked between Penny and Izzy. He jutted his double chins at Penny. "You look like you could do with a bracing walk." He turned to Izzy. "Hop in, thunder hips. Take me to my dog."

Izzy pulled a cringing face at Penny and mouthed, "*Thunder hips*?"

"Are you sure you're happy to travel with this... gentleman?" asked Penny

"I will be fine," said Izzy. "I've got knitting needles in my bag."

"No time for knitting," said Derek oblivious. He opened the passenger door for Izzy, got in and started the car. The engine puttered smoothly into life.

"Purring with pleasure," he said, and before Izzy could catch a final glance of Penny, he had accelerated out, through the yard and down to the gate that led to the main road. He turned left on the main road, heading out of town. He was either ignorant of the local geography or intent on a circuitous route.

En route, Derek kept up a strong one-sided conversation which was made tolerable by the fact that Izzy couldn't hear him particularly well over the wind that whipped by.

"— Monty's absolutely spoiled rotten," he was saying.

"He seems a lovely dog," said Izzy.

"The boy! The boy! Fliss's girl's boy! She and Will are a pair of soppy bleeding heart champagne socialists. Give you the shirt off their back and expect the honest taxpayer to chip in, too. Spoilt the daughter, spoilt the grandson too. Oh, but I see through them. I do. Something not right there. Course, those Mountjoys are even worse in their own way. That Frank... has he ever told you about the time he saved the Woodbridge Under Elevens football team from drowning?"

"Er, no," said Izzy, who had never met the man.

"Oh, he will," Derek assured her. "He will. Ugh, imagine being stuck in the house with the lot of them for a week. Frank, Carmella, Jacqui and me, all guests of the Starlings. They're lovely but it's a blasted relief to get away from the place, spend some time on the road with a sweet chunky saucepot."

Izzy had never been called a chunky saucepot, sweet or otherwise, and she didn't particularly like it. She especially didn't like the fact that it was accompanied by a fat hand squeezing her knee. She prised it away.

"Hands off me, eyes on the road, Sir," she told him sternly.

"Sorry, Matron," he said. "Now, where was I?"

"Telling me how much you dislike the people you're staying with."

He threw her a mad and furious glance, during which the car veered unpleasantly close to the verge.

"Dislike? They're my best friends in the world!" he said. "Never hear a word said against them. We rub along just perfectly. Like a well-oiled machine. Sure, there's something amiss under the bonnet but that's the way of things." He threw her another disapproving look. "Dislike!"

The car rattled at speed down the narrow Pepper's Wash road. Summer greenery threatened to slap Izzy in the face as they sped through.

"Up the market hill," Izzy instructed.

"Yes, yes," replied the florid fellow, irritably. "I have driven round here before, you know."

He braked somewhat sharply outside the Cozy Craft shop.

"Nothing like a run in the country to get the juices flowing, eh?" he said.

"Hmmm. I do feel a bit nauseous," Izzy agreed.

The thought that she might throw up in his car seemed

to spur him into action. He was swiftly out and round her side of the car.

"Open the suicide doors and out you pop," he said.

"Suicide doors?"

He was about to explain when a horrid homunculus with a sagging wrinkly face jumped out at him from behind the nearby phone box and yelled. Derek gave a startled yell of his own and stepped back. The figure, who Izzy realised was not a wrinkly homunculus but a child in a rubber mask, laughed loudly and then ran off.

"Bloody hell!" said Derek. "What was that?"

"A child playing silly beggars," said Izzy, getting smartly out of the car.

"Why was the child wearing a Telly Savalas mask?"

"I think it's meant to be Patrick Stewart. Well, *Next Generation Space Captain*. We used to specialise in non-copyrighted Halloween costumes."

Derek pointed a trembling finger after the lad.

"You sell those masks?"

"We did. We gave them out at Monty's party."

"You gave my dog a party?"

"Monty, Fliss's grandson."

"There should be laws against such things," he huffed.

"Parties?"

"Scary masks."

"I don't think people would normally regard Jean Luc Picard as scary." She tilted her head in thought. "Then again, the mask they used in those *Halloween* movies was just a Captain Kirk mask painted white."

"Really?" asked Derek in the manner of one who simply didn't believe it.

"I think so," she said. "I don't think I dreamt it. They took a William Shatner face mask and, with a spot of paint, transformed it. Wooden actor to stone cold killer."

"Gosh," said Derek, and there was a look of intense thought on his face that a William Shatner trivia fact did not perhaps deserve.

"And now your dog," said Izzy.

She unlocked the shop door and stepped inside to find the playful corgi growling at a tiny footballer figurine on the floor.

"Must have fallen off the cake," said Izzy, scooping it up.

The dog yipped playfully and then, seeing Derek, sprinted straight to the man.

"Oh, Monty, my boy!" said Derek, kneeling to let the dog jump up and lick at his face in delighted reunion.

It was such a simple, sweet and unguarded moment of affection between dog and owner that Izzy forgot for a split second that this was the same man who had groped her knees and called her things she never wished to be called again. But only for a split second.

# 6

When Penny returned to the shop, Izzy was waiting with mugs of tea and leftover birthday cake.

Penny looked at the cubes of dark cake coated in lurid icing. "Why have we still got the cake?"

"Nobody's come to pick it up," said Izzy.

"Doesn't mean we can eat it."

"I don't think they're going to count the slices, Penny."

Penny took a plate and was about to ask whether this was a bit the dog had licked when she realised the dog had gone.

"Monty's gone."

"Along with his owner," said Izzy, evidently glad that this was the case.

They sat on chairs at the side of the counter. Officially, the shop was still open but things were always at their quietest in the late afternoon. The quiet of the afternoon was different to the quiet of the morning. At closing time, with the sun hanging low, there was the feeling of a day's work done. The noise and bustle had been and gone, all construction and creation had reached its conclusion. The quiet of the afternoon was the quiet of baked cakes cooling on the side, the quiet of relaxation after the party guests had gone home. Penny luxuriated in it and, more often than not, she could not think of a better time or a better place to be than here, sharing it with her cousin.

And then, out of nowhere, her mouth still half full with a corner of cake, Izzy asked, "Would you ever describe me as 'chunky saucepot'?"

"Um, no," said Penny. "What is a 'chunky saucepot'?"

"That was going to be my follow-up question."

"Derek Masters?" Penny hazarded.

"Yup."

"It's certainly been an interesting afternoon."

"I don't think I would describe Derek Masters as interesting."

"I mean the dress commission."

"Oh, I know!" said Izzy. "Time to practise painting lobsters."

"And time to start costing up what we should be charging. This shop in Wickham Market Fliss mentioned..."

"The Wickham Dress Agency?"

"Who are they? What do you know about them? Are they competitors?"

Izzy shrugged. "Maybe they are, but I've never really thought about them that way. Nanna Lem never did. They act like they're in London."

"You mean...?"

"Charging fancy London prices."

Penny's eyebrows shot up. "Really? And do people pay them?"

"I guess somebody must. They do the dress exchange thing, so it's kind of like a really posh version of a charity shop, and then they will alter or make things as well. I went in there once and I felt scruffy and out of place. You know some shops where they stare at you to scare you off if you're not rich enough? It's like they have a radar that tells them if you're wealthy. A sort of can-you-paydar."

Penny huffed. "I know exactly what you mean. It's a dreadful way to do business. Why would you be mean to people like that?"

"It's like they've never even seen *Pretty Woman*!"

"Quite." Penny scowled. "We'll concentrate on getting that quote together for Fliss and then maybe we take a field trip over there to check them out."

"Costs all noted for the Lobster Overall," said Izzy, handing Penny a piece of paper.

"Oh, really? Already?"

"Already. You were slow walking home."

"I'm not slow." Penny looked over Izzy's workings out. "Great work, though. Can you really do the painting yourself?"

"Sure. Why not? I'll give anything a go. Except another ride in a car with that Derek Masters. Never again."

"I thought you said never say never."

"Shut up and eat your cake," said Izzy.

# 7

Penny woke to sunlight streaming through the curtains of her small but comfy flat above the shop. When she'd arrived several months earlier, the space had been used as a storeroom, piled floor to ceiling with bolts of cloth, patterns and other sewing paraphernalia. Most of these had now been repurposed, sold on or stood in the corner of the workshop, waiting to be dealt with. There were some absolute gems among them. There was a whole bolt of a Laura Ashley floral print that had been barely touched since its arrival several decades ago. Flannel, taffeta, gabardine, buckram and cotton. All manner of things that had to be moved out so that the little flat could be given the cleaning of its life. With a fresh lick of paint it was now a little space Penny was glad to come home to.

The bed was old and the springs creaked but — Lord, oh Lord — it was comfortable. There were two plush armchairs by the little table beside the window, in which two women could drink an evening cocoa and watch the world go by in the marketplace below. And even though the place was small, it was larger than the pokey rooms she was still paying for in London.

Penny had come to Fram to help out while Nanna Lem was in hospital with her leg. Now Nanna Lem was out and back at her flat in Miller Fields sheltered accommodation, but she had shown no sign of wanting to come back to the shop. With many of Penny's possessions still in London and a hefty chunk of cash going to pay for her rooms there, it was probably time to speak to Nanna Lem about exactly when Penny could give up her role here and return to the city.

Dressed, she went downstairs to prepare for the day. She was mentally planning when she might find an opportunity to visit Nanna Lem when she noticed there was already a customer waiting on the pavement outside. A customer of sorts. It was small and furry with a happy expression that few individuals could muster at this time of morning.

Penny opened the door and the little corgi bounded in and did a few laps of the shop.

"Monty! What are you doing here?"

Monty provided no answers but instead sniffed at the box that had served as his bed for much of the previous day, and then went to explore the rest of the shop. Minutes later, Izzy arrived with a pair of foamy and chocolate-sprinkled coffees from the Dancing Goat café just up the road.

Monty yipped from the back room.

"Did you just bark?" said Izzy, putting the cups down on the counter.

"I did not," said Penny.

Monty came scampering in. Izzy crouched automatically to fuss over him.

"We have a dog again," she said.

"We do," Penny agreed.

"But we gave him back."

"We did."

Izzy gasped and looked at Penny. "Did you fall in love with him and go back and steal him?"

"I did not."

"Because that would be kidnapping. I don't know what the punishment for kidnapping dogs is."

"I suppose you dognap a dog," said Penny.

"Still a serious crime."

"Which I did not commit."

Izzy frowned as she gave Monty vigorous tummy rubs. "Why is kidnap to steal someone but catnap is to go to sleep?"

"Is that really the most pressing question here?" asked Penny.

"It's a good one for my word nerd column in next week's Frambeat Gazette."

Penny clicked her fingers in front of Izzy's face. "Focus. We have a lot to do today. We have a dress to make and we don't need a dog as a distraction."

"No," Izzy agreed. "Well, I can pick up the pattern from the printers any time after nine. Maybe you should take young Monty here back where you got him from —"

"I didn't steal him."

"But he stole your heart, didn't he?" said Izzy in a

deliberately sappy voice. "And while you do that, I will get the printed pattern."

Penny huffed, but Izzy was right. Also, she had a foamy chocolate-sprinkled coffee she could savour on the walk up to Saxtead Grange.

Using a length of braided silver rope she found in the back room as a lead, Penny walked Monty back to his temporary home. She liked the idea of a good walk as much as the next woman, but she hadn't planned on spending an hour of her Wednesday walking a dog. Nonetheless, the sky was blue and the air warm and she couldn't help enjoying the sight of the butterflies fluttering around the hedgerow on the way out of town. As she gazed across a field, she saw a darting movement in the treeline and wondered if it might have been a roe deer, even though she knew that deer would not be out and about so late in the morning.

Walking up the long track to the gateway to the house, she noticed the bright shapes of emergency vehicles.

"What's this, Monty?" she said.

Monty did not have an opinion.

There was an ambulance and a police car parked on the gravel driveway. A man in beige chinos and a shirt and tie was chatting to a policeman in the courtyard. Penny found herself slowing her stride, approaching quietly, as though she was intruding upon something.

The policeman saw her, made an exclamatory noise and jogged over.

"You can't come in here," he said.

"I have a dog," Penny replied, which, she realised, wasn't the most brilliant of explanations. "What's happened?"

"There's been an incident, Miss," he said.

"That's really non-specific," said Penny.

"Do you often come up here?"

"Only when I'm returning dogs to their owners," she said, and felt at once that this was too flippant. "I'm doing some work for Fliss Starling."

"She and Mr Starling are inside, talking to the sergeant. Maybe best if you come back another time."

The man in chinos came over. Penny would have judged him to be somewhere in his sixties or seventies but he held himself erect and unbowed.

"Who is this?" he asked.

There was a jolly pig pattern on his loosely tied tie. "Are you Frank?" Penny asked.

"I really don't know this woman," he said, with the speed of a man who'd possibly had to say those words a number of times in his life.

"You breed pigs," added Penny helpfully.

There was the shout from the house, the same woman's voice that had shouted at Derek the day before. Frank Mountjoy winced visibly at the sound.

"I really must go," he said.

Penny waggled Monty's lead. "But I've got Derek's dog. I was just returning it."

Frank glared at her. There was a wet shininess to his eyes. "Derek is dead," he hissed with sudden emotion.

"I'm sorry?"

"Some b— bloody miscreant attacked him in the garage last night, brained him with his own spanner and then scarpered across the fields."

"Now, sir," the police officer began, "let's not go speculating —"

"Oh, we all know what happened!"

There was another shout, presumably from Mrs Mountjoy, and Frank stalked away with loud and furious footsteps in the gravel.

"You know the people here?" asked the police officer.

"Oh, barely," said Penny. "I was doing some dressmaking for Fliss." She saw the policeman had a notepad in his hand now. "Oh. I've met Fliss and Will. I know that the Mountjoys are staying here. And Derek. Was. Derek was staying here too. They're doing the classic car weekend thing in town. And another woman..."

"Jacqui Bildeston."

"Jacqui. That's it. Wife to Monty. Not Monty the dog," she said and laughed nervously. "Or Monty the boy. The original Monty. She's his wife. Widow. I appear to be blathering."

"You do."

"Oh! And the maid or cook or whatever. Susan. She was here."

"No. She left at six last night, before Mr Masters was attacked." The policeman pursed his lips, conscious he had perhaps said more than he should have. He sucked his lip and sighed. "And you are?"

"Penny. Penny Slipper. I run the Cozy Craft shop in town."

He nodded, as if he had known this already, and was merely testing her. "Right, well, you'd probably best go back. We'll be done here at some point today."

Penny indicated the dog. “But I was bringing Monty back.” She held out the lead to the policeman.

Monty and the policeman looked at each other.

“I don’t think I want a dog right now, Miss,” he said. “Best he stays with you.”

# 8

When Penny re-entered Cozy Craft, Izzy had just returned from the print shop with the printout of the pattern for the vintage overall. She had laid it out on the cutting table, alongside the instructions.

Monty did a circuit of the shop and growled sharply at one of the dressmaker's dummies.

"I can't help but notice that you have returned with a dog," said Izzy.

"Derek is dead."

"What?"

"Derek Masters is dead."

"He can't be. I was only in his car yesterday."

"He's dead. Clonked on the head or something. Some intruder attacked him in the garage and ran away."

"Oh, my. That must be awful for them. For them all. Staying in that house together. Who was there? Obviously, Fliss and her husband, Will."

"The Mountjoys. Frank and Carmella. And then Derek and Monty's widow, Jacqui. Jacqui Bildeston, I think the policeman said."

"Chatting to policemen, were you?"

"It's very serious. A man's been murdered."

"Didn't he have a wife too?"

Penny tried to recall. "Derek, No. Fliss had said she... oh, some old fashioned name. Ethel, Ermintrude — Gertrude! Gertie. She'd said she died, didn't she?"

"Two couples. Two widowed individuals."

"Well, only one now," said Penny. "Derek is dead."

Izzy looked at her patterns. "It kind of puts a crimp on their classic car weekend plans. Do you think Fliss still wants her outfit?"

"We can hardly phone up and ask her, can we? 'Oh, hi. We're making your beach pyjamas and heard your friend died. I know it's a day of grief for you but we really need to know if we should continue.'"

"That would be a bit insensitive, Penny."

"Yes, it would, Izzy. I think we should get on with it and then take the financial hit if she backs out later."

"A very professional attitude," Izzy agreed.

Penny looked over the patterns. "But can we make it in time?" asked Penny. "It's only two and a bit days away."

"The construction looks straightforward. Let's make the toile straight away and then we can get Fliss back for a fitting. When it's sensitive to do so. Then we can divide and conquer. You make the finished garment while I use the toile to practise painting the lobster."

"Yeah, about that. What kind of paint do we need?" Penny asked.

"Fabric paint," said Izzy. "Or maybe we can do it in watercolour and —"

"—Are you about to suggest a dodgy workaround that will leave Fliss with a nasty stain on her garment?"

"Um, no. We'll get the proper stuff," Izzy insisted.

"You know what would be helpful?" said Penny. "We should time ourselves making this commission. It will be helpful for us to monitor how much time we're taking to complete this."

"We could do that, but it will depend which one of us is making it. I will be faster than you, because I have more experience."

Penny smiled. "Then why don't we both make a toile? We'll capture the data for both."

Penny watched a variety of emotions play across Izzy's face. She could see that Izzy thought making the toile twice was pointless, but then she saw that thought immediately chased away by the prospect of a contest.

"Yeah, let's do it!" Izzy hurried off to fetch the calico and frowned. "When do we start timing? Before or after cutting-out?"

"I started it while we were talking. Planning time needs to be included."

"What?" Izzy slammed the calico onto the cutting table, sending the pattern fluttering off. "Quick! Get the paper scissors and cut out the paper pieces. I'll make a double layer of calico so we cut both sets out at the same time."

Izzy ran back and forth like a woman possessed.

"You do know that this isn't a race, don't you?" tried Penny but she could see that Izzy was not convinced.

It wasn't long before they each had their own pile of pieces to assemble.

"Oh, wait, which sewing machines shall we use?" asked Penny. "Some of them go faster than others. We need to make it fair."

Izzy beamed. "I don't think the speed of the sewing machine will make the difference. In fact, I will take the treadle and you take the electric, how about that?"

Penny had heard Izzy brag that she could treadle as fast as the electric machine, but she knew better than to bring it up now. "That works, thanks."

They both settled at their machines and started to put the garments together. In spite of herself, Penny felt drawn into the competitive mood and found herself concentrating hard. She glanced across at Izzy and saw that she was already sewing the first seam. "Oh hey! You haven't even pinned that!"

"No, I know when I can get away without pinning and just hold it in place instead. Did I mention experience?"

Penny wanted to grumble about it not being a fair contest, but reminded herself that it was data collection, not a contest.

# 9

It was just after lunchtime and Penny had carefully pinned her first seam and was about to start stitching it when the door opened and a customer entered. Except it wasn't a customer, it was the man from this morning, the one in chinos and with the pig patterns on his tie: Frank Mountjoy.

"Ah, this is the place," he said, looking about the shop with a certain measure of haughty disdain.

"Good morning," said Penny in what she hoped was either a subdued and mournful tone or at least something broadly neutral. "How are you doing?"

He looked at Penny quizzically and then he noticed Monty sniffing his trouser turn-ups.

"Oh, it's you," he said.

"It usually is," replied Penny.

"You've got Derek's dog."

"Not by choice. Have you come to collect him?"

Frank seemed to recoil. "He was Derek's dog and the rest of us have a lot to process at the moment. I'm sure you understand. The police have been tramping all across the Starlings' property. Laid their grubby hands on certain cars without due care."

Penny might have delivered a biting comment about Frank's priorities, but grief was a strange thing and people didn't always say what they were feeling.

"We're very sorry to hear what happened," said Penny.

"I bet you bloody are," he said, and there was an angry edge to his voice.

"Yes. Yes, we are."

"So, this is where you sell them, is it?"

"Sell them?" Penny gestured to the shop. "Sewing supplies and fabrics. We're making an outfit for Fliss right now. Not sure if she'll still want it but —"

"The masks!" he hissed. "The masks."

"Er..."

"Fliss's girl, Caroline. She had her son's birthday party here."

Penny smiled politely. "She did."

"They all had stupid masks when they left," he said.

"Yes. They were a gift from us."

"Yes. Derek said he was ambushed by Telly Savalas."

"Patrick Stewart," Izzy piped up from her work station.

"He said it was Telly Savalas. Kojak, right?"

"I really wouldn't know."

"I do. It was all he wanted to talk about at dinner,

muttering something about James T Kirk being the killer from Halloween."

"I really couldn't say."

"He did. I had been recounting the story of how I'd saved the Woodbridge Under Elevens from drowning in Fram Mere and he simply came out and interrupted me with this nonsense. Masks! And now I'm worried that Caroline's Monty —"

Monty the dog sat up and begged, tongue lolling.

"Not you. Monty the boy. He's bound to be blamed for the masked crime spree that's sweeping the town."

Izzy emerged from behind her work station. Words like 'masked crime spree' would attract her attention every time.

"I didn't know there was a crime spree," said Penny.

"Well, there damn well is! Ringing doorbells and running away, climbing on things that oughtn't be climbed on and the latest I heard was that a clown was seen jumping out from behind graves and scaring folks over by the church."

"Oh, I see. It would be a terrible thing if young Monty was blamed for such activities."

Frank's upper lip twitched as he grew red with anger. "I like young people. They're the future and all that. Ask anyone. Frank Mountjoy is a big believer in youth. I saved the Woodbridge Under Elevens from drowning in Framlingham Mere some years back. Pulled a dozen soggy tiny footballers out of the muck there. I wouldn't have done that if I didn't love kids."

"Er, no."

"But this crime wave must stop. You must have sold lots of those masks!"

"If they were a bestselling line, would we have given them away?" asked Izzy from over Penny's shoulder.

Penny didn't approve of such bluntness to a customer, but Izzy's point must have sunk in, as the man shook his head and seemed to withdraw. There was now doubt and confusion in his eyes, a moment of weakness.

"I don't know. I even wonder now whether the man I saw was wearing one at all," he said, looking at nothing.

"The man?"

"The man in the field."

"The man in the field?" said Izzy.

"The murderer, damn it!" said Frank. "I saw him."

"Oh."

Izzy and Penny drew together, attentive. Morbid it might be, but it wasn't often one heard about encounters with murderers.

"You actually met him?" said Izzy.

"Saw him from my room. We'd all gone to bed. That was the last I saw of Derek alive, chuntering about William Shatner masks. We didn't know it was the last time we'd see him. We went to bed and I got up a bit earlier than normal. Might have been woken by the dog barking in the yard. Carmella was already up but women are like that, aren't they? Very early risers."

"They can be," said Penny neutrally.

"And I flung back the curtains, and there he was in the field."

"The killer?" said Izzy.

"Doing something odd behind the hedge. Looking out and ducking down. Stupid face. Might have been a Boris

Johnson mask. I couldn't make it out at that distance. Didn't think anything of it until I went downstairs and over to the garage. Flaming dog was yapping at my heels and excited about the garage. The doors were open, see?"

"Yes?" said Penny.

Frank's voice had gone quite soft by this point.

"I have a Triumph Dolomite Roadster. Beautiful thing. It'll be the star of the car weekend. Sure, Will's Bentley is worth a few bob more now he's got it running, but it's a dour and stuffy thing. My car was built for fun."

"You were saying, about going over to the garage," Penny prompted with involuntary interest.

"He was there. Derek. On the ground between his Midget and Will's Bentley. The spanner beside him."

"That's terrible," said Izzy. "We're so sorry."

"Maybe he interrupted a burglar. Any of those cars would be worth a pretty penny. I hollered. I yelled. Someone called the police, I suppose."

He frowned intensely and then he seemed to remember himself. He drew himself up, any softer emotions erased from his face.

"You and your bloody masks," he said, accusingly. "You need to think before you act, don't you?"

Penny said nothing, even though the masks and the murder clearly had nothing to do with one another.

Frank stalked stiffly to the door, but then turned.

"I don't know why Fliss came to you for a dress." He cast about disparagingly. "This isn't a patch on my wife's shop."

With that, he was gone. Neither Penny nor Izzy said

anything. Eventually, Monty broke the silence by barking at a dust mote drifting in the sunlight.

"There's a man with a lot on his mind," said Penny.

"Apparently, we're not a patch on his wife's shop."

"I heard," said Penny, nodding thoughtfully. "I think I need a cup of tea."

"I know what you mean."

# 10

As the day progressed, Penny noticed a buzz around the town. They'd had a flyer through the door to say that the cars taking part in the car show would be put in place from Friday when the roads would be closed to traffic, but there was already a greater volume of people around than usual. A marshal visited the shop to politely remind them that any deliveries would need to be rescheduled if they were due for the weekend.

"I don't know whether to be excited," Penny remarked to Izzy. "It's not as if I'm mad about cars."

"Yeah, I know what you mean," said Izzy. "It's that passion that people have though, isn't it? It doesn't matter what the subject is, when people really geek out about a thing, it's sort of infectious."

Penny nodded.

In between bursts of work on the toile, Penny had tried to glean what she could about Wickham Dress Agency,

Carmella Mountjoy's shop. The website, however, was so very sparse that it seemed almost deliberate. A banner across the top declared that it was Suffolk's best kept secret.

Izzy came and peeped over her shoulder. "Is that Audrey Hepburn?"

"I think it must be a lookalike. Audrey Hepburn looked like that many years ago." Penny had to concede it was a great photo though. The photograph showed Audrey Hepburn, in full *Breakfast at Tiffany's* splendour, standing outside the door of the shop looking enthused about something just inside the door.

"There's no actual information about what sort of shop it is," complained Penny.

"Part of the mystique, I guess," said Izzy with a shrug. "I see they have a late night opening on Wednesdays if you wanted to go and check it out tonight."

"What? I'd have to be some sort of super-competitive weirdo, or maybe a massive nosy parker to want to do that!" replied Penny.

"Yeah, I know! We'll go after we close up here then, shall we?"

Penny wanted to protest that she was neither competitive nor nosy, but she knew it would be a lie. "Fine. But how will we get there? You can ride your bike but I haven't got one."

"Taxi it is, then," said Izzy. "But I've got an editorial meeting of the Frambeat Gazette at half five."

Penny considered the time. "We shut up at five. We'll both head over to Miller Fields. Your meetings never last more than an hour. I'll pop in and see Nanna Lem. Then when you're done, we'll taxi over to Wickham Market and a look at this shop."

"Is this what they call industrial espionage?" asked Izzy conspiratorially.

"We're not spies," said Penny firmly. "We're not enemies. Wickham Market is a whole other town. Two towns can have two dress shops. We can even be supportive of one another."

Izzy tapped the side of her nose. "Great cover story. I like it."

# 11

The British summer was not always a dependable thing but, as Penny and Izzy closed up for the evening, there was golden sunshine and a rosy warmth to the evening air. They strolled together across the cobbled marketplace, through the Crown Inn and out through the rear courtyard that led directly onto Fore Street.

Miller Fields was a relatively modern sheltered accommodation complex, set back from the road and surrounded by trees. Nanna Lem had been living there for a few years and, coincidentally, it was where the editing team of the amateur local newspaper, the Frambeat Gazette, met on account of its editor in chief also being a resident there.

Penny parted with Izzy at the entrance and went round to Nanna Lem's flat. She rang the bell and she was buzzed in.

"I wasn't expecting you today," came her grandma's voice from her little living room.

"Am I interrupting your hectic schedule?"

"Don't be cheeky. *House of Games* is about to start on BBC2 and I like to see if I'm cleverer than the celebrity contestants."

Nanna Lem had lived in a number of places during her life. Many years ago, she'd apparently lived in the flat Penny now occupied, back when Cozy Craft had been her own grandmother's shop. As a married woman, she'd lived in one of the Swedish houses on Dennington Road before widowhood and old age had led her to reconsider her living arrangements. Across the years, she'd accumulated all manner of possessions but not all of them had made it into this current flat.

Nanna Lem's living room was dominated by a deep, cushion-strewn sofa. Nanna Lem perched at one end, almost as though the armrest support was the only thing stopping the sofa from swallowing her whole. By the side of the sofa was a square wicker basket full of knitting yarn and needles. Beyond that was a table piled high with magazines, some whole, many gone but for the patterns removed from them. The pile must have been two feet high, and Penny imagined a team of fashion archaeologists might spend years researching the mysteries lying within its depths. Nanna Lem herself was currently hand-sewing the edges of what appeared to be a very small dress.

"Are you sure you've got the measurements right on that?" asked Penny.

Nanna Lem held it up. The dress was no more than eight inches tall. "Imelda Green in sixteen B wanted a new dress for her panda."

"That makes perfect sense now you've explained it," said Penny.

"Toy panda."

"I hope so."

"You putting the kettle on?"

Penny dutifully went to the small kitchen and put on the kettle for tea. She automatically did a bit of washing up while she was there.

"We're gathering some toys and oddments together for the tombola on Sunday," said Nanna Lem.

"Tombola?"

"We're having a fete here to coincide with the second day of the car show. A sort of an open day for potential future residents to look round."

"That's nice."

"Not sure I enjoy the implication that there will be space here for them. It does rather suggest we current residents are not long for this world. Think you can rustle up a toy for us?"

"Should think so," said Penny, squeezing and removing tea bags.

"So, to what do I owe this honour?" asked her grandma.

"Can't I just come and visit my favourite nanna?"

"So, no reason?"

"Maybe a reason."

"First, tell me how my shop's doing?"

As Penny brought the teas through, removing a purple wool felt hat from the sofa so she could sit down with her grandmother, she recounted the recent doings of the Cozy Craft shop. Nanna Lem hadn't visited the shop once since her return from hospital but seemed to revel in Penny's descriptions of what was going on there. Penny had learned that Nanna Lem enjoyed the tiny specifics. Penny told her about the latest stock they'd ordered. She told her which of the few regular customers had come in to buy what fabrics. She'd even brought along some of the newer patterns they were selling for Nanna Lem to look at.

"You heard of Wickham Dress Agency?" Penny asked.

Nanna Lem scoffed, nearly sloshing her tea.

"Carmella Mountjoy's place."

"That's the one."

"Not a patch on our shop."

"Huh. Funny. Her husband said something quite different."

Nanna Lem gave her an irascible scowl. "What are you doing consorting with those types?"

And so Penny told her grandma all about the lobster beach pyjama commission and the car show at the weekend and the news that Derek Masters had been murdered.

"Fliss Starling said that Derek's wife had spoken highly of our shop."

Nanna Lem made a very visible effort to remember.

"Ah. Gertie Masters. Yes, I did know her. Only slightly. I made a number of items for her. Oh, that must have been at least ten, fifteen years ago. Died in a car crash."

"That's sad."

Nanna Lem nodded and adjusted her bad leg on the pouffe it was resting on.

"One of them classic cars so it had no seatbelts or air bags or anything. Must have been this time of year because I think it was just before the motor show weekend. It wasn't her behind the wheel. It was another feller's car. Monty someone."

"Monty Bildeston?" said Penny.

"Could be. Aren't that many Montys about, are there?"

"Funny you should say that, I've met a couple this week," said Penny, not mentioning that one was a boy and the other was a little dog. "So, Gertie Masters and Monty Bildeston died in a car crash together, did they?"

"That's right. Coming into Fram one Saturday, took a corner too quickly. Rolled into a field. Killed em both instantly."

Penny thought on that, huffing steam from her still warm tea. Derek's wife and Jacqui's husband killed in the same crash, a double tragedy for the friendship group.

"A bunch of odd characters, that lot," said Nanna Lem. "The Starlings have that big old place up near Saxtead, don't they?"

"They do."

"That Will seems nice enough but the rest of that crowd... Ugh. The Mountjoys are perfectly horrible people. Don't go having anything to do with that Wickham shop. Why would you care what's going on in Wickham, eh?"

"Well, you've got me looking after the shop, Nanna. If I'm to continue then maybe I need to check out the competition."

The older woman grunted at that and then, ignoring the hint, waved at her telly. "Look, *House of Games* is coming on. Richard Osman. He's dead clever, in't he?"

"In terms of running the shop..." Penny prompted, deciding only the direct approach would work.

"Yes?"

"Are you likely to come back soon?"

"Soon," said Nanna Lem breezily.

"You don't have to hurry but I'm still paying rent in London and if I knew how long..."

"I don't want to stop you getting on with your life..."

"No, it's not like that. I'm just..."

"I'll be back at the shop soon enough. It's just my leg..." She shifted her bad leg a little more and pulled an uncomfortable face. "When it's healed properly..."

"And I don't want to rush you."

"I don't want to be a burden on you, Penny."

And the discussion on the shop and how long Penny would be staying petered out as, on the screen, the host welcomed his celebrity guests to a half hour's worth of brainteasers and puzzles.

# 12

Izzy was at the editorial meeting of the Frambeat Gazette. It always took place in the Miller Fields community room so that Glenmore Wilson, a resident in the sheltered accommodation, could easily preside over the meeting in his capacity as editor in chief. The Miller Fields management knew they'd get no rent from the Gazette but tolerated their gatherings nonetheless, knowing full well that the Gazette operated on a shoestring, and that paying for nothing that could be scrounged for free was the only way to ensure its continued survival.

The editorial team of the little paper consisted of Glenmore, Izzy, Annalise from the town library and Tariq, who was working with them as part of a university placement.

"Listen up, people," said Glenmore, who might have been an old man now but who still had some of the disciplinary fire he'd picked up in a career in the military. "We have lots to get through this time, as we will need to plan the content for the souvenir edition featuring the car show."

"The souvenir editions are really popular," said Annalise. "You might want to put this in your uni portfolio, Tariq."

"Yes, yes, yes." Glenmore huffed with impatience. "I was going to mention that. In fact, I have some good news for you, Tariq. You've mentioned on numerous occasions that you want a press pass, yes? Well, I have acquired for you something even better. It's a VIP press lanyard for the motor show. It's access-all-areas for every single moment."

"I didn't know any areas of the car show were off-limits," said Tariq.

"It's a very public event," Glenmore agreed.

"So, access-all-areas... doesn't really mean anything?"

Tariq was perhaps young and a little naïve, but he was no fool.

"But this lanyard will set you apart, mark my words," said Glenmore.

Tariq picked it up and read from it. "It says *Ask me to take your picture!*"

"Yes!"

"Surely this is just a lanyard saying that I'm there as an unpaid photographer?"

Izzy smiled, happy to see that Tariq had cottoned onto what the role entailed.

"If you came into journalism expecting a life of glamour or gratitude then you must know by now that you were mistaken," rumbled Glenmore.

Tariq snatched the lanyard. "I didn't say I wasn't going to do it, did I?"

"Very good. You'll need to make sure you cover all of the major areas of the programme, of course. I shall take pictures of the cars myself, as I shall be writing a little critique of what I see."

Tariq nodded. "You're a fan then?"

"Oh very much so!" said Glenmore. "I love a classic car. Nineteen sixty-six, I set my heart on buying a brand new Hillman Hunter. That was just before I signed up for Her Majesty's army. I never got to buy one, but I still love a well-preserved car. Properly preserved. I don't have any time for the more peculiar things that turn up, mind. They'll let all sorts enter the show, for novelty value I suppose."

"Novelties?" said Annalise.

"Frankestein's monsters," muttered Glenmore, darkly.

"Oh, with modifications, you mean?" asked Tariq, as he scanned the list of categories.

"Tsk! A modification is one way to describe it. Abomination is what I'd call some of those things! Shoehorning this engine into that car, just to see if it will work!" Glenmore had become animated, waving his arm around as if to demonstrate that the secret behind such things was sorcery rather than simple motor mechanics. "And then to top it all they'll spray the damnable thing with metallic paint or give it pink fluffy upholstery! At least it means we can see the beastly things coming."

Tariq was confused by the outburst. "So if there's cars like that do we include them?"

"Oh yes, of course we do," huffed Glenmore. "We try to get a picture of every car into the souvenir edition. Even the rotten ones."

"Right," said Tariq.

"Now, we'd better move on to news and features," said Glenmore.

"Who's covering the masked menaces?" asked Annalise.

"What's that?" asked Glenmore, reaching for his glasses.

"An actual honest-to-goodness menace. Children wearing masks have been terrorising folks."

"Not seen them," said Glenmore.

"I don't suppose they've been able to get in here," said Annalise. "We've had them in the library, running in and out during story time."

"That hardly sounds like terrorising," Glenmore grumbled.

"Pelting the windows too, with stuff out of the bins. It was very alarming for the younger children."

"Do you have any pictures?" asked Izzy.

"We do not!" said Annalise. "Our library is very tidy and clean. The last thing we want is for pictures of it looking messy to go viral."

Izzy wasn't certain that the sight of a soggy teabag sliding down a window was enough to make Framlingham library go viral, but she nodded in sympathy.

"I got a picture," said Tariq.

They all turned to stare at him.

"It's not great, because it took me a bit by surprise." He held up his phone to show a picture of a miniature Donald Trump skateboarding on the pavement outside Mr Chan's Chinese restaurant, as an elderly woman whirled aside in alarm.

"Goodness me!" exclaimed Glenmore. "That is a very good picture."

Izzy nodded. It was rare to hear Glenmore praise anyone's efforts, but Tariq's photograph had captured a highly dramatic moment with great efficiency. The crouched figure on the skateboard was on the one hand youthful and athletic, but also featured the gross, distorted face of the disgraced former president. The old woman looked truly afraid as she toppled to the side, and all of this had played out in front of a well-known landmark.

"Someone needs to find that woman," barked Glenmore. "This can go on the front page if we can write it up with a victim statement."

"I've seen her," said Annalise. "Her name's Lilian or Lilibeth or something. Teaches woodwork at the college."

"Start there, Tariq. Hunt her down! In the meantime, everyone send any more mask-related leads over to Tariq. You're on point for writing this up, my boy. I hope you're up to the task!"

Tariq slapped a hand against his chest as if pledging an oath. His face was alight with possibility. "Yes! Yes I am."

"Jolly good," said Glenmore.

Izzy could already picture him sketching out the headline *Tiny Trump Terrorises Town Technology Teacher*. At least no one had yet mentioned that the masks had come from the Cozy Craft shop.

# 13

On the taxi drive over to Wickham Market, Penny posed a question that had been bothering her.

"Did you know that Derek's wife, Gertie, and Jacqui's husband, Monty, died in the same car crash?"

"You mean they ran into each other?" said Izzy.

"No, they were in the same car which went off the road."

"Oh."

"This was years ago. I was just thinking... if a man and a woman who weren't married to other people were in a crash together..."

Izzy could clearly see where Penny's mind was heading. "You think they were having an affair?"

Penny heard the tone in her voice. "I'm being silly, aren't I?"

Izzy tutted. "Can't two people drive around together without being in some sort of relationship?"

"Sorry. Sorry."

Izzy looked out at the red summer sky. "I mean that's absolutely where my mind went when you first said it."

"Is it?"

"But we're jumping to conclusions."

"You're probably right."

Izzy patted Penny's leg excitedly. "So, what's our game plan for the reconnaissance mission then?"

"Game plan?"

"Yeah! Are we going to go into Mrs Mountjoy's shop and pretend that we're millionaires who like to dress down, or what?"

"We don't need to pretend to be anyone, do we? Why can't we just go in there and look round?" asked Penny.

"Not sure that will work," said Izzy. "It's research, yeah? We might need a cover story to justify our questions. How about we're personal shoppers for an unnamed celebrity?"

"Can't we just reach out in a friendly manner and tell Carmella Mountjoy we have a shop in Fram? Don't you think there's more to be gained from collaboration?"

Izzy gave her a very doubtful look. "Well, maybe."

Wickham Market, a small town similar in size to Framlingham, seemed a less busy place than Fram. That could be because it was later in the day of course, thought Penny.

They stood for a moment outside the shop, examining its exterior. It wasn't such a characterful building as Nanna Lem's shop. It was probably of a similar age, but it was two storeys, not three. The signage was subtle but enticing. It was the rich purple of a chocolate box. The window display featured a pair of mannequins with a soft grey curtain behind them. Raised platforms showcased handbags and accessories. The mannequins both wore brightly coloured cocktail dresses, and Penny looked carefully to see if there were prices shown, but she couldn't see any.

"So, I'll wear the green one, you take the red one," said Izzy, pointing at the dresses.

"I wonder how much they are?" Penny mused.

"Dunno, but that looks like a Hermes Kelly bag," said Izzy, pointing. "They go for thousands."

"Let's go inside and have a look." Penny pushed open the door.

The interior was darker than Penny had expected. The lighting was subtle and there was thick carpet underfoot.

"Good evening, ladies!"

The tall slender woman at the counter wore a dress with a tiny matching jacket in salmon pink. She held a champagne glass in one hand, sipping convivially with a woman on the other side of the counter who was dressed in a sixties-style mini dress featuring a bold hexagonal print. There was a tray of glasses on the counter. Perhaps this was a feature of late night opening?

Penny and Izzy approached, but there was no offer of a glass.

"Um, I'm looking for a dress," said Izzy.

"Yes?" said the slender woman. Her silver hair was cut in a sharp and stylish bob.

"Something for the Fram motor show," Izzy continued.

"This shop sells vintage couture garments," said the woman.

"Yes," said Izzy.

"It is perhaps worth your while becoming acquainted with some of our prices."

Penny could have laughed at the icy response. Izzy smiled, and showed no sign of being affected by the implication. Penny wasn't sure whether Carmella would be manning her shop personally on the day one of her social circle had been murdered, but if this frosty stick of a woman was indeed Carmella then Fliss's comments about the woman's contemptuous attitude were accurate.

"Thanks," said Izzy. "I'll just browse then, shall I?"

She approached a rail of clothes and pulled out a dress that featured splashes of green and blue. She held it up against her body. "What do you think, Penny?"

Penny walked over to look, acutely aware of the woman staring at them both. "It's nice. Is it your size? Maybe you could try it on?"

"That is Balenciaga," said the thin woman. "I'll ask you to treat it with care, as the silk is very delicate. I believe the price on that dress is nine hundred pounds."

The message was clear. She wanted Izzy to put it down, but Izzy, who was able to ignore social cues with ease, walked over to the centre of the room to examine the dress in better light. "Nah, it doesn't really scream motor show, does it?"

"Well, what would?" asked Penny.

"I think there are two possible approaches," said Izzy. "There's the retro fashion approach. The cars are classics, so the fashions should be too. The other approach is to consider the practicality of walking around for hours in the sun. Breathable, easy-clean garments make sense."

The woman walked around the counter making tutting

sounds. "Practical? Did I just hear you utter the word practical?"

"Maybe?" said Izzy.

"You must cast aside such dreadful constraints! It's what's wrong with the world today. Fashion must never be hidebound by such nonsense. Now, does this garment speak to you or not?"

Izzy looked thoughtful. "It does, but I think I'd need it to speak a little bit louder for nine hundred pounds. We'll keep looking."

The woman sashayed back to the counter and engaged in low murmuring conversation with her friend. They glanced up every so often, not bothering to disguise the fact that they were discussing Izzy and Penny.

Penny flicked through a rack herself. It was surprising how few racks there were in here. The lack of variety in the sizes on offer was also noticeable. Sizes below the average were plentiful; anything above was scarce or non-existent. Carmella and her friend were thin to the point of being cadaverous, so perhaps only skinny rich people were welcome here.

Penny paused when she came to a dress. It was a very simple sleeveless design, with no embellishment, but it was shocking pink on the left and lime green on the right. "So, I could make something like this, could I?" she asked Izzy.

"You definitely could," said Izzy and then waggled her eyebrows playfully. "In fact, you should."

"What kind of fabric is this?" Penny felt it, and found it had a very subtle bounce between her fingers, although it was dense and definitely woven.

"Wool crepe," said Izzy. "Not cheap stuff, but you'll love wearing it."

"That is Dolce & Gabbana, ladies," said the woman. "Twelve hundred pounds. Please take care not to mark it. It's very pale, you see."

Penny didn't know what she hated the most. Was it the way she was being made to feel like a sticky-fingered child who would smear mess onto the nice things? Was it the fact that the woman felt the need to explain that it was pale? Mostly it was the way she had decided, as soon as they'd walked through the door, that Penny and Izzy were a nuisance rather than potential customers.

"Hey check this out!" called Izzy. She lifted a parasol from an ornate umbrella stand and opened it out, exposing its fluttering lacy panels.

"Nice," said Penny.

"Please don't open that in here!" the woman said sharply from the counter.

"Oh, is it the bad luck thing?" asked Izzy. "I know a lot of people get superstitious about opening umbrellas indoors."

"No, it is because that is a genuine vintage Bohemian parasol and I don't want to see it damaged."

Penny prided herself on remaining composed at all times, but this woman was really testing her. "How will you sell it if nobody can see what it looks like?"

The woman laughed. "Oh, my dear thing, I could sell a hundred of these if I had them during the week of the motor show. Lots of moneyed folks all wanting a cute vintage accessory. It's a snip at two hundred pounds."

Izzy folded the parasol and placed it back in the stand.

"Well, I must thank you for letting me look at it. With my eyes."

Penny turned. "Excuse me. Can I ask, are you the owner?"

The woman raised her chin to present her face more fully. "I am. Were you hoping to speak to my manager?"

"Carmella?"

A high forehead creased in a frown.

"I just wanted to express my sympathies. About what happened this morning?"

The woman looked genuinely non-plussed for a good few seconds before realising what Penny was talking about. "Oh. Oh, yes. That. Very sad. Can't even step out one's own front door without being attacked."

"Yes, very sad," said Penny. "Izzy and I met Derek briefly."

"Yes. He knew a lot of... ladies," said Carmella. "The whole thing has made me question staying so near to Fram. Big town, rough elements."

The notion that Fram was either a big town or had some sort of major crime problem was laughable. Penny said nothing, and she and Izzy left. Both of them wanted to breathe the clean air outside.

As they stepped out on to the pavement, Penny pulled the door shut slightly harder than necessary. "That was weird."

"I know! Who says 'with my eyes'?" Izzy said with a sorrowful shake of her head. "I don't know what came over me."

"No, I mean Carmella. If Derek was her friend then she was taking his death very calmly."

"Posh people do hide their emotions."

"No, I think she's probably a monster."

"Penny Slipper!" said Izzy, shocked.

The more Penny thought about their encounter with Carmella Mountjoy, the more she could feel herself going red in the face with annoyance.

"That woman was absolutely beastly to us," she said and then clamped her lips tight as she realised someone had just emerged from a polished saloon car outside the shop.

"I'd like to say that she's lovely once you get to know her," said the man as he eased the car door shut.

Penny swallowed hard, embarrassed that she'd been overheard.

"What do you mean you'd like to say that?" asked Izzy. "I feel that there's a second part to your sentence that goes something like 'but I'd be lying.'"

The young man raised his eyebrows. "I couldn't possibly say such a thing about a customer."

He wore a blue and white pinstripe suit. While the suit was perfectly tailored to his physique, he was so boyishly young looking that it still seemed over-sized for him, as if he were a child playing at being an adult.

"Customer?" asked Izzy.

Penny saw that the man carried a large briefcase, embossed with a gold logo, too shiny to make out at this angle.

"Fabric supplies," he said.

"I thought they just sold clothes," said Penny. "I didn't see any signs of actual dressmaking."

"Ah, yes," he nodded. "They're like swans."

"They can break a man's arm with a swish of their wings?" said Izzy.

The man gave a smile. It was a nervous thing, like he wasn't used to speaking to everyday people. "Majestic and serene above the water, busy working below the surface. They have a workroom in the back where they do alterations and fixes. I supply fabrics and haberdashery."

Penny frowned. "We run the sewing shop in Fram. How come I've never seen you?"

"Our company doesn't deliver outside of London, normally," he said. "When Mrs Mountjoy relocated here we carried on the service as a special favour to an old client. I mean, if your shop is near to here, I could always drop in while I'm in the area, although our stock is kind of pricy."

Penny thought for a moment. "Do you have any wool crepe?"

He nodded. "I could bring some by in the morning? Framlingham, you say."

Penny smiled. "That would be great, thank you!" She looked at the business card that he had pressed into her hand.

*Oscar Connelly representing Silken Threads.*

"Wish me luck in there," he said with a dramatic waggle of his eyebrows.

# 14

Bright and early on Thursday morning, Penny took their new lodger, Monty, for a walk. She didn't necessarily consider herself a dog person. She regarded it as virtually impossible to be a dog person in bustling, urban London. London was a city of rooftops and alley cats and Penny struggled to understand how people who lived in busy cities could ever own dogs, animals that demanded green open spaces. Now she was living in green Suffolk, perhaps she would discover if she was a dog person herself.

She took Monty down Bridge Street and through the car park to Framlingham Mere. The mere was an interesting feature of the landscape. Sitting in the broad hollow beneath the imposing edifice of Framlingham Castle, the mere was simultaneously meadow and lake and what proportion of it was meadow and what proportion of it was lake fluctuated greatly depending upon time of year and weather. Right now, the lake had retreated to the centre and the grasslands about it were sufficiently dry that a woman and her dog could trot round without getting too muddy.

A herd of cows grazed contentedly on the far side among the tall grasses and meadow flowers, and in this semi-rural quiet, Penny could easily imagine that this was the very same scene her medieval forebears might have gazed upon: nature, agriculture and castle.

Frank Mountjoy had said he'd saved a children's football team from drowning in that mere. That would have been a sad and terrible death if not for his intervention. Blustering self-important pig breeder the man might be, but a hero was a hero, she supposed.

From the mere, they walked up the path to side of the castle. The jagged wall of the twelfth century fortification rose high up to their left as they circled round onto the castle road and back down through the town.

There was a familiar figure up a ladder in Double Street. Aubrey Jones was applying cheery Suffolk pink paint to the walls of a house, covering up the more lurid colours beneath. He'd started that job months ago but there had been peculiar legal wranglings following the owner's death.

"Finally getting it done?" Penny called up to him.

Aubrey grinned down at her. "I see you still have a dog."

"He's growing on me," said Penny, and Monty yipped his approval. "I haven't yet thanked you for helping out with the birthday party."

"No thanks needed."

"Maybe treat you to a pint at the Crown?" she suggested.

"I will not say no to that," he said.

"Tonight?"

"It's a date," he said and then checked himself. "I mean, I mean it's a pint."

She laughed at his awkwardness, waved him farewell and left him to his work.

By the time she was back at Cozy Craft, Izzy had arrived. Breakfast was put down for Monty, morning coffees were drunk and the challenge of sewing the toiles for the overalls resumed.

An hour or so later, Penny looked up and saw Izzy manipulating something that looked like a nearly-finished garment, while Penny was still wrestling with the lapped seams which were new to her, although Izzy said they were used a lot in the thirties to accommodate the fun geometric shapes that were a feature of the era.

"Finished!" shouted Izzy. "Well, apart from the hand sewing."

Penny gave her a haughty look. "So, not finished."

Izzy huffed. "Fine, I'll do that too."

Penny wasn't even certain where the hand sewing was. She looked over to see that it was on the inside, to fasten the lining down to the bodice. Izzy would have that done in a few minutes. She resolved to keep going. She was the tortoise and Izzy was the hare.

Izzy bounced off to iron her toile and Penny started the long vertical seams of the trousers.

"Oh hey! Look at me!"

Izzy strode in, wearing the toile.

"That is for a customer!" said Penny. "Not for playing with."

"We have two! Or we will have, eventually," said Izzy.

Penny just smiled. "That does look amazing. I knew the trousers were wide, but they aren't just wide, they are massive, in a really good way!" The bodice was a neat fit, with shoulder straps and a flattering panel at the waist, and the dramatic flare of the trousers lending the garment its vintage character.

"I like the Wonder Woman panel at the waist," said Izzy.

Penny smiled. It did have a superhero feel, the way it pointed up at the centre.

"It's gorgeous. It might be nice to keep these toiles for afterwards," said Izzy. "I mean, calico's a practical fabric, yeah? We can wear them for gardening."

"There's no garden here, Izzy, although I agree with the sentiment."

"Meh, we can get a windowbox just so we can wear these." Izzy mimed watering flowers in the style of a thirties starlet.

"Mine will be done in an hour or so, I think," said Penny. "Time to find out if Fliss still wants her beach pyjamas, or if death has put a dampener on the weekend's plans."

She was tempted to simply text to ask, but she knew that was the coward's choice. She steeled herself, and dialled Fliss's number.

# 15

From listening to Penny's side of the conversation, Izzy picked up that Fliss Starling was adamant she still wanted the painted lobster outfit. While Izzy waited, she consulted the internet on her phone. She didn't consider herself a morbid creature, but still found herself searching for details of the car crash that had killed Gertie and Monty. There was an older news article and a picture of the wrecked vehicle itself. If not for the description giving the make and model, Izzy wouldn't have been able to confidently identify the mess of red-painted metal and rubber as a car, let alone a nineteen thirties Bentley.

Since she was being nosey, she also searched for news of young footballers rescued from the mere, and found a much smaller article in the archives of a local newspaper site, that simply stated that a Woodbridge youth football team had got into trouble while crossing the mere one evening and that a passing motorist, Mr Frank Mountjoy of Wickham Market, had pulled one boy from the lake and led the rest to safety.

Penny put her phone down.

"Fliss wants to try on her toile?" said Izzy.

"She'll be here within the hour."

"Time to tidy up then?"

There was the jingle of the shop door opening. Monty perked up in his box bed and sniffed the air.

The slight but very smart figure of Oscar Connelly entered the shop, bearing his case of fabric samples. He smiled at the two women and then cast about his surroundings.

"Now *this* is charming," he said.

"Morning," said Izzy. "And thank you."

"You found us all right?" asked Penny.

"Prime position in the marketplace. Delightful setting. How have I not visited before?"

"I couldn't possibly say. Cup of tea?"

"Do you have Earl Grey?"

"We can look," said Izzy, who knew that the kitchenette upstairs held a treasure trove of random teas, half finished packets of biscuits and unmatched tea cups. The chance of there being Earl Grey was high. The chance of the tea actually being in date was lower.

As Penny went off to look, Oscar commented, "She's not local, is she?"

"Originally," said Izzy. "We're cousins. But her family moved up north and then she went to London and now she's stuck here helping me."

"Just herself?" he asked, trying and failing to sound casual. "No, um…?"

"Boyfriend? Girlfriend? Et cetera?" suggested Izzy, smiling.

The poor man's face was an absolute picture. He truly was a cute and innocent boy decanted into a man's body.

Penny soon returned, teas were poured and they all sat on stools at the cutting table as Oscar spread out some samples.

"You were interested in wool crepe?" he asked. "I've brought some for you to look at."

Izzy and Penny spent a pleasant few minutes going through the samples. They were generous pieces, which allowed them to get a sense of the drape as well as the feel of the fabric.

"I thought I was allergic to wool for years," said Penny. "I remember complaining about it being scratchy but this is so smooth, it's gorgeous." She slipped it over the back of her hand. It seemed impossible that this was related to some of the coarse fabrics she remembered from the skirts of elderly aunts.

"Some wool fabric is scratchy," said Izzy. "I'm sure Oscar was about to tell us about the different kinds of sheep and other animals and how the fibres are all different."

"I really wasn't," said Oscar, looking terrified at the very idea.

"Oh. I was looking forward to seeing pictures of the sheep."

"Izzy's only teasing," said Penny. "At least, I think she is. These fabrics are delightful. Expensive though, I bet?"

Oscar pointed at the sticker in the corner of the sample.

Izzy knew that Penny would be speechless at the number written on it, so she chipped in. "I have an idea. We need to know if there's a demand for fine fabrics like this in our shop. Sell us a couple of these sample pieces, Penny can create a stunning dress and then we'll see if we get a lot of interest."

Oscar shrugged. "I can leave a couple of these samples behind, free of charge."

"Really?"

"Does that work for you?"

Penny picked up what were clearly her favourite pieces. She ran them through her hands with a delicate sigh and grinned widely. "Thank you so much, that would work beautifully!"

After Oscar had packed away his remaining samples and finished his drink, Izzy couldn't help herself. "So what did Carmella order from you?"

"Izzy! It's probably not appropriate to talk about someone else's business," said Penny.

Izzy smirked, because Penny's face did not match Penny's words. Even Oscar seemed to realise that Penny was curious too.

"Well, I'm not due back in London until tomorrow," he said. "I'm booked into this delightful hotel by the River Deben but I have no evening plans."

"Really?" said Izzy. "I don't believe Penny does, either. The Crown across the way serves a lovely dinner."

"What?" said Penny, taken by surprise.

"Oh, I wouldn't want to impose," said Oscar.

Penny's face stuttered from one expression to another as her mind scrambled to keep up with what was going on.

"I mean, yes," she said. "That sounds great. Dinner with a fabrics rep would be a great opportunity to discuss..."

"Fabrics," Izzy prompted.

"Fabrics," said Penny. "And the state of the industry."

"And maybe what other persons are getting up to," said Izzy.

"Er, maybe," said Oscar.

The door rang again. Fliss Starling entered.

"A customer," said Oscar. "I've taken up enough of your time."

As he hurriedly gathered his spare samples, Fliss made tiny gestures which presumably were intended to convey that he need not hurry.

"Seven o'clock?" he suggested to Penny.

She nodded eagerly and he backed out, doing a nervous involuntary hat tipping gesture even though he wore no hat.

"What a smart little man," said Fliss, amused, when he had gone.

"Can we just say how sorry we are to hear about Derek," said Penny.

"I've heard a lot of sorries and deepest sympathies today," replied Fliss. "All well meant, I'm sure. Will is parking his monstrous car as we speak. Have you really finished the garment?"

"The toile," said Izzy. "Just to try on so we can check the fit."

She picked up her calico creation and sent Fliss to try it on.

# 16

Penny had her timer running while Izzy and Fliss were discussing the fit of the outfit. She didn't think she was being overzealous in adding this to the overall cost of the dress creation. Time was time, and if they were to be paid appropriately for their services then every minute spent working on this specific request counted.

As the seconds ticked by on her phone, the shop door opened and Will Starling entered, wearing his driving gloves and his slightly preposterous newsboy cap.

He looked about and gave her a look that was both amused and confused at the same time.

"I thought I saw my sugarplum come in here. Can there be two dress shops on this street?"

"No, she's here," said Penny. "I'm Penny. We met the other day."

He looked at her wide-eyed.

"Left my glasses at home. So we have. Where is she, then?"

"Just trying it on."

"Going to cost me the earth this thing, eh?"

Penny glanced at her timer. "Craft costs money."

He chortled. "Tell me about it. Doing up Monty's old car and —"

Monty the dog yipped from his basket. Will looked at him in surprise.

"Not you, Monty," he said and then frowned, not in confusion this time but in sudden if mild distress.

"I'm very sorry to hear about Derek," said Penny, assuming the distress was linked to the animal's owner.

Will simply stared at the dog.

"Is it right?" he said.

"Is what right?" asked Penny.

"It's only been a day since... since..." He held himself still for a long moment. "Irritable bugger. Really he was. Wasn't really a friend of ours. I mean he was, obviously, but it was Gertie who brought him to the friendship group and stuck him there. He was just this thing that turned up uninvited each Christmas, like the smell of sprouts. I don't wish to speak ill of the dead..."

"No, no. It's fine," said Penny.

"He wasn't my friend. I can't say I cared for the man. Or his dog, really. Sorry, old boy. But he's dead and we move on. Is it right?"

"That's... that's death, I guess," said Penny.

"Ah. Ah, true." He looked at Penny now and there was a moist glint in his eyes. "You get to a certain time of life and you end up going to more funerals than weddings. Last wedding was our Caroline's. Course Derek was there for that one. Very generous with gifts he could be. Also a very affectionate man in his own way."

Penny remembered Izzy's account of the ride home from Saxtead Grange and said nothing.

"And yet it comes to an end so suddenly. There we were all having a perfectly pleasant dinner and we all go to bed and the next thing I know is Fliss is shaking me awake to tell me that Derek is dead."

"I certainly had to wake you," said Fliss, emerging back into the shop proper wearing the toile. "Frank was yelling fit to burst. Good job one of us is a light sleeper."

"Let me pin the hem up," said Izzy, following behind, "so that you can properly see how the trousers fall."

A few moments later, Fliss swished up and down. "This is a really lovely choice."

"Yes, very nice dear," said Will.

"I'm so glad I asked you two for help. I can't wait to see the final version in linen, although I do rather love this one in a wholesome sort of way!"

Izzy inspected the fit and made a couple of tiny adjustments. "Let's talk about where the lobster should go. We could pencil it onto this if you like?"

"Lobster?" asked Will.

"It's a Dali thing," said Fliss.

Izzy and Fliss stood in front of the mirror adding curves to the calico to show where the lobster would go.

"All very good," said Penny, still watching her timer.

"Right," said Fliss. "I'll go and take this off now."

The two women disappeared again.

"Money's no object, you know," said Will, his voice dropping to a sort-of-conspiratorial whisper. "The dress. We'll do anything to make our loved ones happy, won't we?"

Penny nodded and then mentally cast about for a topic of conversation.

"So, you're working on Monty's old car, you say?"

"Restoring it," he nodded. "A labour of love. It's like a ten thousand piece jigsaw and half of the pieces are bent out of shape."

"Oh. It's the car in which..." Penny stumbled over how to say, 'it's the car in which Monty and Gertie, possibly in the midst of an extra-marital affair, met their untimely ends.'

"It is that car indeed. Classic Bentley. He had it painted a delicious red. Not unlike a lobster, actually. Wonderful car. Bentley owner myself so I know a thing or two about them. But it's been a long old process. Jacqui's keen to see it done. A source of many happy memories for her."

"And sad ones too, surely," said Penny.

"That's life, I suppose. It's all a rich mix, all manner of tangy flavours."

"Quite right," said Penny.

Fliss was soon back. "Are you sure you will get the proper version finished in time? We've barely got a day left."

"It's our top priority," said Izzy.

"Absolute stars, the pair of you."

"Aren't they just, my love," said Will and offered her his arm as they left the shop.

# 17

Just before lunchtime, Izzy held up the toile, now with a vague lobster shape sketched onto it.

"I might make a start on the painting. I'll make a tiny adjustment to the pattern based on the fitting then you're good to crack on with making it up with the linen, yeah?"

"I am," said Penny. She was getting better and better with the sewing and looked forward to working with the smooth, crisp white linen.

Penny was also keen to put her unexpected gift of fine fabrics to good use. The samples that she had kept from Oscar were not the same colours as the fun dress she'd seen in Carmella's shop, but they were clashy and fun together in a similar way.

"How can I make a start on this dress?" she asked Izzy.

"Look through the patterns for a simple shift dress. Shout

me when you find one, I'm just popping over the road to get something. Back in five."

Penny wandered over to find a pattern. Izzy had explained the mixture that existed in the world of patterns. The large established pattern houses worked from the catalogue system, and the shop would top up its supplies of each pattern as they sold them. What Izzy called the Indies were patterns that were produced by independent pattern makers. Each producer had a range with its own personality. They mostly came in nice quality envelopes with quirky illustrations on the front.

Penny started with the catalogues. It was certainly easy to choose, as she could just flick through to the dress section and page through lots of different designs. It was a beguiling experience, something like clothes shopping but with almost infinite possibilities given the mixture of patterns and fabrics that surrounded them.

Penny was so absorbed with her task that she paid no attention to Izzy's return until she heard a loud clatter. She walked through to see what was happening.

"What's this?" she asked.

"Malibu Sunset paint," Izzy told her, taking a small tester pot out of her pocket.

"I meant the huge bundle of brollies under your arm."

"I went to the charity shop and bought a load of umbrellas," said Izzy proudly.

Penny looked down at the motley selection scattered across the counter. "Right. Fine. I can see that. Not sure I understand. I thought you were painting a lobster. Are you starting an umbrella museum? Or is very bad weather forecast?"

"No, no. This is more fun than that. It's going to be great. You heard what Carmella Mountjoy said, right? During classic car week all of the rich folks will be wanting to buy cute vintage accessories like a parasol? Well, we take these old brollies and we swap the boring waterproof parts for cute vintage frilly parts. Genius, yes?"

"Goodness me, that is a fun idea. They won't be real vintage, though."

"I am not sure that Carmella's are either. She said the one I was looking at was from Narnia!"

"Bohemia."

"Even worse. Everyone knows that was a Queen song, not a real place."

Penny knew that wasn't right, but it probably wasn't an important point.

"Let's give it a go, shall we?"

"You need to practise painting lobsters," said Penny. "I need to get on with Fliss's final outfit."

Izzy pouted but could see the sense in Penny's words.

# 18

Izzy hung the beach pyjama overalls from a shelf so that she could look at the reference lines for the lobster, but she made her first attempts on paper. She'd ordered some fabric paints, but for getting the design right she was using the matchpot of Malibu Sunset she'd picked up from the hardware shop while out buying umbrellas.

It was a bright orange colour, and was meant for painting walls, but Izzy needed to capture the basic lobster shape.

Izzy enjoyed sketching, especially in the style of fashion illustrations, but painting was less familiar to her, so she expected that it would take a few attempts to get things right.

She closed her eyes and pictured the lobster. She was certain that moving forward with confidence was the key here. She loaded her brush with orange paint and made a bold curve on the paper. It was a good start. Probably. The colour was good. She would worry about the head and the tail once she had the middle in place. She added legs, and then quickly used her phone to double-check how many legs a lobster was supposed to have.

"Ten! How can that be right?"

"Eh?" Penny looked up from sewing the overall.

"Lobsters have ten legs. Who knew?"

"Two of them are the big claws at the front, I expect," said Penny.

"Um. Yes, of course." Izzy licked her thumb and used it to try to erase the extra pair of legs she had added. It was not successful.

She sighed and found another sheet of paper. This time she would not walk into any obvious traps based on the weird anatomy of lobsters. She used the pencil to outline a body, then the two big claws, and then she counted out eight spindly legs. She started to add the coloured paint to bring the shape to life. Each pencil line got paint, sometimes a little more than intended, but she was on a learning curve, so that was fine. She stepped back. No.

It looked like roadkill. She had, perhaps, created the shape of a lobster that had been flattened with a steamroller.

She grabbed a third piece of paper and went back to sploshing the paint directly in place, now that she was becoming more familiar with what lobsters looked like. A banana shape for the body, some sticking-out legs inside the curve. She added an antenna coming down from the head, but the paint splodged, so she turned it into a front claw, but of course it was much too long.

Izzy stepped back and took a critical look at what was possibly her best effort so far.

"Bagpipes. I have painted orange bagpipes," she murmured. She looked up and forced herself to smile at Penny.

"How's it going?" called Penny.

"Oh, it's coming along," said Izzy. "Coming along."

"I am timing you, you know."

"I'm taking a mental break from the lobster," Izzy declared. "Might try making a parasol."

"Fine. But I'm timing that, too."

# 19

Penny watched as Izzy took apart the first umbrella.

"We need to keep these little plastic things that go onto the end of the spokes for when we put it back together. It's fairly simple sewing to construct the cover, just a load of triangles. See the existing cover? There are a couple of points where the fabric is stitched to the frame, but once I undo that, we can use it as a pattern to make our parasol."

Soon they had separated the hardware from the fabric panels.

"I'm going to cut one out from the white linen offcuts from the beach pyjama overalls," said Izzy. "I'll add lace and some other stuff too."

Penny rummaged through the offcuts and remnants with a smile. "Are you going for subtle and understated, or full-on fabulousness?"

"I'd say that the world of parasols welcomes every possible combination. Let's go wild," said Izzy.

A couple of hours later, Izzy was parading up and down the shop with her parasol above her head, dipping and twirling it in a display that was somewhere between Mary Poppins and a burlesque dancer.

"That looks great!" said Penny. She had discreetly timed Izzy's construction. "How much should we charge for it?"

Izzy shrugged. "It's a one-of-a-kind Izzy special," she said. "From Bohemia or Narnia, whichever makes it the rarest. Twenty quid?"

"You've spent two and a half hours on it," said Penny firmly. "Your time is much more valuable than that. Not a penny under seventy."

"Let's pop it in the window and see if it sells. I'm going to make a colourful one next."

Penny smiled. Izzy valued the fun factor of a given task much more highly than the sordid business of actually making money, but the shop would only succeed if they managed to combine the two.

"Back to lobster painting," Penny commanded, and sent Izzy back to her work.

By mid-afternoon, Penny had almost finished the overall in the white linen. It looked superb! It was softer than the calico toile, but once it was pressed it had an immaculate crispness. She put it onto the mannequin and stood back to admire it.

Where was Izzy? Probably still practising painting lobsters. She'd moved upstairs, claiming that she couldn't concentrate with the ins-and-outs of customers.

Penny trotted up the stairs into the workshop space. Every surface was covered with paper daubed with orange paint. Izzy stood in the centre like a whirling magician creating more and more of them. Penny gazed around at her various efforts. Maybe these were early attempts and Izzy had got the hang of it since, as nothing she could currently see particularly resembled a lobster. Penny looked at more and more of the paintings. Some were hasty and splodgy, some were more carefully executed, but lacked any sense of proportion. The one thing that they all had in common was that they were terrible.

Izzy finally looked up and met Penny's gaze. Her face was contorted in despair. "You know, these words do not come easily to me, but I think I might have bitten off more than I can chew. I have discovered that I cannot paint a lobster."

Penny walked into the room and gave her a hug.

Izzy sobbed loudly. "I'm sorry!" she wailed. "I thought I could do it! I always think I can do things. Sometimes I'm right, but not today."

"Don't worry," said Penny patting her back. "We'll think of something."

Penny composed a text to Aubrey, painter and decorator. Painting was painting, she supposed. If he could paint houses then surely he could paint lobsters.

We have a situation. It's not as urgent as the cake being eaten by the dog, but it's more urgent than the dent in the skirting board. Hard to explain. Can you call in?

# 20

When the shop door next opened, Penny looked up, expecting — or rather *hoping* — to see Aubrey, but instead a uniformed police officer walked in. It might very well have been the one Penny had met outside Saxtead Grange yesterday morning. Much to her shame, she realised that the only thing she remembered of that particular officer was his uniform, as if the bright hi-vis jacket and bulky utility vest had blanked out any more personal details.

"Morning, Ma'am," he said, and then glanced at the clock and corrected himself. "Afternoon. I wonder if I could ask you a few questions."

"Yes?" she said, suspecting the questions weren't going to be about doing repairs on his uniform or asking what style of stab-vests might be in this season.

"Do you sell masks?" he asked.

"Ah. I see. I know what this is about."

"You do?"

"Come to arrest us for starting a crimewave carried out by our army of miniature mask-wearing miscreants?"

"Er, no," he said. "And have you started a crimewave carried out by an army of miniature mask-wearing... what was it?"

"Miscreants. Um, no. We haven't. I don't know why I said that. Masks, eh? We used to sell them, but we've got rid of nearly all the fancy dress stuff now."

"I see. When did you get rid of them?"

"Earlier this week, mostly. We gave some away after a child's party."

"Ah, yes," he said, pulling out a notebook and consulting it. "And might one of these masks be of the former Prime Minister Boris Johnson?"

"Ah," she said, understanding.

"Ah?"

"This is about the murder."

"Suspected murder."

"Is there some doubt as to whether he's dead or not?"

"The deceased is very much dead. The circumstances are still being investigated. And how do you know about the former prime minister's involvement in this?"

"Something Frank Mountjoy said. He saw someone in a field."

The policeman sighed. "I see."

"He came in here to... I don't know if he was accusing us."

"He was!" called Izzy from the back room.

"I think he thought it was one of our masks the attacker wore. Chances are it wasn't actually a Boris Johnson mask.

They really were of very poor quality and it might have been any celebrity of the last forty years."

The policeman took a moment, presumably to consider what celebrity might bear a passing resemblance to the former prime minister, and then looked at his notebook again. "And it seems the deceased had spoken the night before he died about a killer wearing a William Shatner mask."

"Captain Kirk?"

"Or TJ Hooker, if you wish."

"What killer?"

"That particular matter was not clear."

Izzy came bustling through from the rear and treated the police officer to a brief if peculiar lecture on the identity of the killer from the old *Halloween* horror films.

"And it was a William Shatner mask?" asked the policeman.

"In the film. Painted white," said Izzy.

"Is that relevant?" said Penny.

"Can't see how," the copper admitted. "And is there anything else you think the police might want to know regarding this matter?"

"Derek Masters called me a sweet chunky saucepot," said Izzy.

"And we've got his dog, Monty," said Penny.

"Who's named after a man who died in a car crash with Derek's wife."

"And is any of that relevant?" asked the policeman.

"We wouldn't know," said Penny. "We're not trained police officers."

He considered this and then slowly closed his notebook.

"Thank you for your help," he said, and ambled out. In the doorway, he had to squeeze past Aubrey coming in.

"You're here!" Penny said.

"You asked," he replied.

"Come upstairs and we'll explain."

Aubrey was soon standing amongst the dozens of failed lobster paintings while Penny explained the commission and Izzy stood nearby looking miserable.

"Have I told you before that I'm a fan of the interesting pickles that you two get into?" Aubrey said. "Life is never dull in this place. I'm honoured that you've asked me for help, but you do know that I'm the sort of painter that very much has an implied 'and decorator' after his title, don't you? Clients rarely come to me for fine art."

Izzy strode forward and put a paintbrush into Aubrey's hand. "Here. Give it a go."

She pointed him to a blank piece of paper and showed him the printout of Dali's work on the Schiaparelli dress as a reference.

Aubrey dabbed the brush into the paint and made some experimental marks on the paper. "I didn't expect to be copying a Dali when I got up today. I must say that this room is lovely and light for working in."

Penny beckoned Izzy to the door. "We'll get the kettle on. Shout if you need anything."

"Soya milk in mine," said Aubrey.

"Please give it your best shot."

Back in the front of the shop the two of them conferred in whispers.

"What if he can't do it?" Penny said.

"He will. He has to," said Izzy. "Let's get one of the toiles. If he can do it on paper then we need to get him confident that he can paint it on fabric."

Penny was about to get one of the toiles when she was distracted by movement outside.

"Who's that?" asked Penny. "Someone keeps walking past and looking through the window, but they haven't come in yet."

They both watched as the person made another pass, and this time they saw her face, sharp features outlined by a silver bob.

"It's Carmella Mountjoy!" said Izzy.

As all three of them locked eyes, Carmella stopped walking and made an elaborate pantomime of noticing the shop. She stepped forward to look at the display in the window, and then finally pushed the door open and walked in.

# 21

"Good afternoon," said Penny.

Monty yipped a greeting.

"Well, well," said Carmella. She looked them both up and down, and then turned to scrutinise the shop and its contents. "This place is like stepping back in time."

"Do let us know if we can help you with anything," said Penny.

Carmella whirled to face her. "Don't think I don't know what you're up to! If last night's little visit was an attempt to steal my best ideas, then at least I know I have nothing to worry about." She picked up a recently finished parasol from the cutting table and dropped it with a disdainful expression.

"Take care of that!" said Izzy. "It's from Gardenia."

"Ridiculous girl. Gardenia is a flower," said Carmella.

"Ah yes, named after its country of origin."

"What?"

"The Democratic Republic of Gardenia. It probably didn't exist as a country back when you were a schoolgirl."

Carmella rolled her eyes, and then moved along the table. "Well, this looks familiar." She picked up one of the samples that Oscar had left behind and glared at them both. "Poaching suppliers is very poor etiquette. Very poor."

"They are suppliers, not secret agents," said Penny. "Perhaps you're being a little over-dramatic?"

"Over-dramatic?"

"Yes," said Izzy. "It means being more dramatic than is generally necessary."

"I think I am showing admirable self-restraint. First of all, you come sneaking round my shop, pretending that you like dresses —"

"But I do like dresses," said Penny.

"I'm actually wearing a dress," said Izzy and gave her a twirl.

"Fashionable dresses," said Carmella.

"This is what all the Gardenese women are wearing this year."

"— and then my supplier informs me that you accosted him outside and mentioned that you have a fabric shop. And here I find parasols. Parasols like mine!" She spat the word with such venom that Penny took a step back.

Finding herself on the back foot — literally on her back foot — Penny shook her head and stepped forward again, back into the space between them.

"We did not accost Oscar. He introduced himself after we had stepped out of one of the most toxic retail environments I've ever set foot in."

"Penny!" said Izzy, surprised.

"Well," said Penny, with weary annoyance, and glared at Carmella. "You didn't know who we were, but you thought you knew enough to have decided we weren't worthy of being in your shop. What a dreadful way to conduct a business! If you think we're trying to copy you, then you are very badly mistaken. We treat customers well in this shop!"

Izzy gave a discreet clap at Penny's outburst, but Carmella didn't even flinch. She stabbed a finger at Monty in his basket.

"You were at Saxtead Grange on Tuesday, weren't you? And yesterday morning!"

Carmella had turned her attention to the mannequin which was wearing the linen beach pyjama overall.

"Well, what's this? A thirties garment in white linen. I wonder who commissioned this!"

Penny opened her mouth to mention client confidentiality. Carmella huffed so violently that Penny was reminded of a bull about to charge. "Did you find Fliss Starling outside my shop as well? Do you just lie in wait so that you can steal my business?"

"That's quite enough!" said Penny. "We did no such thing. Fliss came to us."

"And you took advantage of her grief to bump up your prices, I bet." A peculiar wave of expressions crossed Carmella's face.

"You all actually seem to be taking it rather well," said Izzy.

Carmella snorted. "Oh, the man was insufferable. And I say that with nothing but affection," Carmella added, and it did seem she was trying to be charitable towards the dead. "He was a proper Lothario. That's a Shakespearean reference," she said to Izzy, assuming her to be stupid.

"I know what one of them is," said Izzy. Penny hoped Izzy wasn't going to mention the 'chunky saucepot' thing again.

Carmella fingered the edge of the linen overalls with contempt. "I'm actually surprised Fliss isn't more upset."

"Why's that?" asked Penny.

"Oh, think it through! There are rumours. But Derek definitely had his eye on Jacqui of late." She humphed, a sort of cold laugh. "Always with the wandering eye. I wouldn't be surprised if Derek's behaviour had driven Gertie into Monty's arms."

The dog barked.

"Not you!" Carmella seethed. "And I suppose Derek, tiny-minded fool that he was, thought that if Gertie and Monty died in that crash together then it was only fitting for the widowed man and woman to come together. Jacqui never saw it that way."

She let the overalls drop from her grip.

"They were arguing at dinner," she said.

"The night before he died?" said Izzy.

"Badgering her with questions until she told him to leave her alone in no uncertain terms."

"Fascinating," said Penny.

Carmella seemed to recollect herself, and realise she had been unburdening herself to strangers.

"And in the morning..." said Penny. "Frank said you were already up when he awoke."

"Yes?"

"So where were you?" Penny didn't add 'at the time of the murder' but it was hard to resist.

Carmella frowned. "I'm not sure what it has to do with you, but as it happens, I was out on the rear lawns having an early cup of tea while this silly dog played havoc in the flower borders. I met Jacqui on the stairs. Had a jolly chat with her about picnic things before I went to get some peace and quiet before the whole zoo awoke."

At that moment a customer entered the shop. Penny took it as her cue to demonstrate what good customer service looked like. "Good afternoon, how can I help you today?"

It was a young woman. "Oh, hi. I just started sewing because I love watching Sewing Bee on telly."

Behind her Carmella tutted audibly.

"I need a zip," said the customer. "Do you have one that is thirty-one centimetres long?"

Izzy stepped forward. "Let's go and check out the zips, shall we? What you probably want to do is get one that's thirty-six centimetres and shorten it slightly."

"Can I do that?" she asked.

"Yes. You can either leave the end hanging down if it's not too much or just chop it off if it's a nylon zipper. I can show you a secret tip as well if you like. The chopped-off part can be scratchy, so I normally wrap it with a small scrap of fabric and machine it down neatly."

Izzy and the young woman disappeared to look at zippers.

Penny turned back to Carmella. "See? That young woman will get great value from her visit today because we took the trouble to understand what she's doing and used our skills to help her though it. She is much more likely to come back with repeat business or sign up for a workshop."

"Nonsense!" said Carmella. "She's almost certainly bought all of her supplies off the internet. She'll pick your brains so that she can go back home and make use of the zip she already has. That's ten minutes of your time she's wasted. Do you know what that is worth?"

Penny was stung by Carmella's barbed question, because it sounded like something that Penny herself would say to Izzy.

"There's more to dressmaking than turning a profit," Penny said, which was equally odd to hear because that was definitely something Izzy would say to her.

Carmella wagged a finger at the linen overalls. "Betrayal. That's what this is."

Carmella turned to the door and stalked out, but not before sticking a hand out to send the parasol skimming across the cutting table and clattering loudly to the floor on the other side.

She left through the door and slammed it shut with an impact that made the entire frontage wobble and had Monty scurrying behind the counter to hide.

Penny released a long slow breath and hoped that Izzy and the young customer had been so wrapped up in their zip conversation that they hadn't witnessed Carmella's fury.

# 22

After the customer had left, spending the grand sum of three pounds twenty, Izzy said, "We should check on Aubrey. See how his lobster work is coming on."

"We should leave him be," replied Penny. "Let's give him time."

Penny needed to lay down the law. Time was very short and everyone was feeling the tension.

Penny forced herself to return to the catalogues to find a pattern for a dress to make with Oscar's fabric samples, but her brain was freewheeling. They had never made a commission that involved fabric painting before, and it was an interesting departure. It was a shame that there was a skills gap, but hopefully Aubrey would be able to help with that. She wondered whether a new children's workshop could combine sewing and painting. Something like a bag just begged to be painted, or maybe even potato printed.

"Penny, Izzy, come and check this out," called Aubrey after a while.

They both trotted up the stairs to see what he'd done. He was working on paper, and several earlier attempts lay on the floor, but the one that was on the table was extremely good.

"Oh Aubrey, that's such a great job!" said Penny.

"Good work with the legs," agreed Izzy.

Aubrey had succeeded in showing the essence of the lobster with relatively few brush strokes. The legs were not all carefully painted, it was more like he had hinted at where they were, and yet it looked exactly like a lobster. "How do you even do that?"

Aubrey gave a modest smile. "I know my way around a paintbrush. This is a fun challenge, actually."

In Penny's eyes, the lobster was a success. It was not quite a Dali, but it had a jaunty character all of its own.

"It reminds me a bit of the lobster in The Little Mermaid," she said.

Aubrey looked mildly embarrassed. "Sebastian? Yeah, it was a favourite of mine when I was young."

"Let's see how it transfers to the fabric," said Izzy.

"Won't we need to use a different sort of paint?" asked Aubrey.

"Yes. We're waiting on a delivery," said Izzy.

"Huh. Best hope it turns up soon then," Aubrey pointed out. "The roads will all be closed tomorrow morning for the motor show. There won't be any deliveries after that."

"And Fliss will be coming for her finished dress in the morning," said Izzy.

"We're cutting it fine," Penny agreed.

"And I really have to get that house finished on Double Street," said Aubrey. "So I can offer you only limited time in the morning."

Izzy checked her phone and nudged Penny. "You need to get changed soon."

"Huh?"

"You're off to the Crown."

"You buying me that pint?" asked Aubrey.

"She has a dinner date," said Izzy.

"Dinner date?"

"It's not a date," said Penny.

"With Oscar Connelly of Silken Threads," said Izzy.

"He's in a band?" said Aubrey.

"A sales rep," said Penny and then to Izzy. "Oh no! I totally forgot that I promised Aubrey we'd go for a pint."

"It was only a pint," said Aubrey, trying to sound indifferent but, in Penny's opinion, not succeeding.

"But a promise is a promise," she said.

"I don't think we even agreed on a date."

"You and Aubrey can have your date tomorrow," Izzy suggested.

"I mean it's not a date..." Aubrey cut in.

"But it's important," Penny insisted. "It's..." She gave an embarrassed and tight smile to Aubrey and said, "Excuse me. I need to have a quick word with my cousin."

She pulled Izzy back through to the shop. She opened her mouth to speak, considered that Aubrey might still be within earshot and then dragged her out of the shop itself, onto the pavement, and shut the shop door firmly.

"Why in the blue blithering blazes did you say I was going on a date in front of Aubrey?" she hissed.

"Cos you are," suggested Izzy.

"It's not a date. It's just dinner with a sales rep."

"Sorry. I didn't realise you had already organised a date with Aubrey."

"That's not a date either!"

Izzy's brow creased. "So, you're going out on non-romantic dates with two separate men for perfectly socially acceptable reasons. The two events don't have to coincide and neither man had claimed dibs on you or anything."

"Blokes don't claim dibs on women," Penny snapped.

"Exactly! So what's the actual problem here?"

Penny struggled to find the words, mostly because the words needed to be based on thoughts and Penny wasn't overly sure what her thoughts on the matter actually were. She spoke as the thoughts came to her.

"I like Aubrey," she said.

"Good. Understandable. He's tall, broad-shouldered and good with his hands."

Penny tutted. "He doesn't worry about life. He goes with the flow. He laughs and he makes me laugh."

"That's almost a list. Have you been doodling your names with a love heart round it?"

"Shut up, Izzy. I like him but I haven't..." She waved her arms around. "... I've not made any moves yet."

"Oh, I've noticed that. I've seen pandas move faster in the romance stakes. So, that's fine. But I warn you, I think Oscar has taken a shine to you too."

"You don't know that."

"He very unsubtly asked me if you had a boyfriend and that."

"And what did you tell him?"

Izzy's eyes sparkled. "So, you're interested in him too?"

"I can like who I want to like."

"Of course you can. Admittedly, he's not tall and hunky like Aubrey."

"No one uses the word hunky anymore."

"You know what I mean. Smartly turned out, though."

"He seems a very interesting man," said Penny. "And he took the effort to ask me out."

"Is that all anyone has to do to win you over? Literally ask? That's a low bar."

"I like it when people show an interest in me," she sniffed. "I'm only human."

Izzy shrugged. "So, we've gone from having two non-dates with two men you're not interested in, to wanting to go on two dates with two blokes you might be interested in."

"I'm not going to be two-timing anyone."

"You do what you like. Be free, cousin of mine."

Penny's brain was a bubbling pot of thoughts and feelings.

"I could actually strangle you sometimes," she said.

"But you secretly love me," said Izzy.

Penny huffed some more but it didn't seem to be achieving anything.

"And that business with the Republic of Gardenia earlier. I know what you were doing but I have to tell you that Bohemia is an actually real place."

"Really? Where is it?"

"I dunno. Poland or Austria or somewhere."

Izzy nodded, pleasantly surprised. "Fine. I do read books, you know. Frambeat's Word Nerd corner columnist, me," she said, and led the way back inside.

# 23

An hour later, with Aubrey gone but having promised to return in the morning if the fabric paints turned up, Penny was dressed for her dinner with Oscar. Izzy made a show of checking how Penny looked.

"Cute top with a flattering sweetheart neckline. Check. A little glow of blusher on those cheekbones. Check. A tiny sillage of perfume. Check."

"Izzy, you're winding me up before what is strictly a regular dinner! Anyway, what on earth is a see-arge?"

"Stop mangling a beautiful word! Sillage is a French word that describes the discreet cloud of perfume that envelops the wearer."

Penny smiled and repeated it. "Sillage. Nice word. Did you use that in Word Nerd Corner?"

"A while ago, yes. Had a couple of farmers write in to the

letters page that I'd spelt silage wrong, but that's what you get for living in a rural community."

Izzy's role at the Frambeat Gazette had many facets and Word Nerd Corner was just one of them.

"Silage is some sort of manure thing?" Penny ventured.

"It's when farmers cut grass for their animals and then they ferment it. It's like sauerkraut for cows."

Penny pulled a face, and Izzy could tell that she wasn't quite sure whether to believe her or not. Her doubts didn't get voiced though, because at that moment Oscar turned up outside the shop.

He was wearing a shirt and tie, which Penny found unusual for evening attire, particularly on a younger man. Smart, attractive but not usual. He smiled at her as she stepped outside. The wattage of the smile went up and down continuously as though he was uncertain which level of smiling was most appropriate.

"You must feel like you live in that shop," he said, looking up at the old edifice.

"Oh, I do," she told him. "Got my own little rooms on the top floor. It was meant to be temporary but who knows how long I'll be here."

They walked together up to the Crown hotel. Old McGillicuddy and Timmy still sat in the centre of the marketplace, watching the sun set over the roofs of the town. The old man waved. Penny waved back.

"For someone who's here only temporarily, you seem to know everyone," said Oscar.

"Timmy and Old McGillicuddy? They're sort of like fixtures."

"Timmy looks a happy, well-looked-after boy," observed Oscar.

"The dog's not bad looking either," said Penny.

During evening, the lights came on over the ground floor windows of the Crown. At this time, the Crown and the Indian restaurant nearby were the only establishments open. Oscar had booked a table which was a good thing as, with the car show coming up this weekend, the town was busier than usual.

Over brie wedges, fish cakes and a bottle of white that Oscar picked, they gave each other their own potted histories. She, Penny, was a local whose family had moved north to Nottingham, only for Penny to find a job in hospitality in London, at a hotel between Hyde Park and Regents Park, a job that had ended spectacularly badly (for reasons she chose not to go into) at a time when her Nanna Lem was in need of someone to help out at the shop. He, Oscar, was a boy from rural Berkshire with a post graduate qualification in Fashion from Edinburgh and who had, in one form or another, worked in fashion and fabrics ever since.

"I think Mum and Dad were moderately horrified that I was going into fashion," he said.

"Is that so?"

"Mum felt I was just trying to send them a coded message that I was gay."

"Right, and...?"

"I wasn't. I'm not. I mean it wouldn't normally be anyone's business but since this is..." He waved a pale hand between them. "In fact, can I ask you a rather personal question?"

"You can ask," said Penny, chasing crumbs of fish cake round her plate.

"This..." He did the hand gesture again. "I wanted to see you this evening because you struck me as a very interesting person who I would like to know better. Personally. Not officially."

"I'd worry if you had an official interest in me," she said.

"I struggle to find the words sometimes," he said.

"Would it be terrible if I enjoy watching you struggle?"

He smiled again, the uncertainty never leaving his smile although its presence was increasingly fleeting.

"So, on the one level, this is a personal dinner rendezvous," he said.

"We can use the word 'date' if you like."

"Not too American a phrase?"

"I think the cultural needle has moved far beyond that point. Let's call it a date."

"Yes."

"Or simply refer to it as 'that nightmare dinner out' if it all goes spectacularly wrong."

"Agreed," he said in his precise tones. "So, on the one hand, this has all the hallmarks of a date and yet..." He pulled an uncomfortable face.

"You're married?"

"No."

"Engaged?"

"No."

"Dying?"

"Please."

"Sorry."

He adjusted his cutlery. "As I'm over here on work business, I do have the option of submitting tonight's meal as an expense. A client dinner, if you will."

"Ah," said Penny, understanding. "So, you're worried that if you pay for all of this on expenses, it will zap any sense that this was a romantic date?"

"Quite," agreed Oscar. "Plus it puts us in that whole socially problematic hetero man paying for the dinner kind of area."

"Hetero man. Sounds like a superhero name."

"I dread to think what his super powers would be."

Deciding she'd finished her starter, Penny swirled her wine gently in her glass.

"So, basically, either you don't put this on expenses, and we split the bill, but definitely maintain all the magic sparkle of a romantic date, or you *do* put it on expenses, I get a free dinner and we have to live with ourselves in the knowledge that our first, possibly only date, was paid for by Silken Threads fabric suppliers."

Oscar visibly re-ran the words through his head. "Yes," he said.

"Mmmm, tough call," said Penny. "Am I an absolute monster if I say a free dinner trumps magic sparkle?"

Oscar smiled with relief. "No. God, no."

"Super," said Penny and drank her wine.

It was only during the main course (Penny was eating deliciously aromatic sea bass with a bacon and samphire medley) that she managed to steer the conversation round to the Wickham Dress Agency and its owner, Carmella Mountjoy.

"Silken Threads have been providing her with fabrics for years," said Oscar. "She previously ran a very successful shop in Knightsbridge and then moved the business up here when she married whatsisname."

"Frank. So, they haven't been together for years?"

"Years, yes. Decades, possibly not. I think their friendship goes back a long way and there might have been exes on both sides. I don't delve, but I do know she moved out here to the country to make a life with a pig farmer."

"Some people might find that a difficult thing to adjust to," observed Penny.

"Oh, I can see the charms of the country life," he said and raised his glass. If that was a cheesy attempt at a compliment, Penny decided to gloss over it for both their sakes.

"He's a successful man, though," said Penny.

"A dreadful boor to talk to," said Oscar.

"So far I've only been treated to the short version of his 'how I saved a drowning football team' anecdote that he apparently tells everyone."

Oscar grinned at that.

"So, the business," said Penny. "The fabrics they order..."

"I would never dream of being indiscreet," said Oscar, "but I can perhaps help you understand how some of our other customers interface with our business."

Penny liked the use of weasel words. *'I will tell you what they ordered, but only if we all pretend that this is an anonymous example.'*

"That would be very kind of you," said Penny formally.

"They recently bought some silk organza. They use it when they revive some of the older garments that have gone a bit limp, it's like an invisible support. Then they always order acetate lining in several colours. The other thing they often buy is tulle. They spruce up hats with it."

"Spruce up hats?" Izzy said.

"Add little veils. They make fascinators too."

Penny nodded. "Interesting. So — and I'm not the dressmaking expert in our team — that sounds like materials they can use to make old tired garments look fresher and newer."

"Restoration work," said Oscar, putting a gentler spin on it. "Despite Carmella's manner with some people, she has a genuine love of clothing."

"It would be nice if she shared that a little more. Everyone and anyone should be allowed to enjoy fine clothes."

"I could not agree more," said Oscar. "Trust me, it was not easy being the only boy in your school who gets excited by a fabulous printed fabric."

He put his knife and fork down on his plate. A good portion of his dinner remained uneaten.

"You didn't like it?" she said.

He tilted his head. "I stop eating when I'm no longer hungry. I used to think that was perfectly normal but it turns out that it's an unusual habit."

"Keeps you trim," she noted.

He tucked at his trouser waistband. "Trousers from Henry Poole of Savile Row, tailors to Napoleon the Third. Don't think I can afford to go up a size. Dare we risk a dessert?"

"I thought you said you were full."

He made a comical frown. “I find that mains and desserts seem to go into separate stomachs, don’t you.”

“Wine too,” she said and drained her glass.

“Want to hear something mildly scandalous?” he asked.

“Who can say no to that question?”

Oscar leaned forward. She leaned forward to meet him. The yellow lamplight reflecting in the hotel window also glinted off his combed blond hair.

“That story Frank Mountjoy tells everyone,” he said.

“Yes?”

“It’s not true.”

“Not true?”

“Well, not true in the way he says.”

“Oh?”

“Carmella told me a different version once, when she was feeling — hmmm, let’s say vindictive — and you must never repeat this to anyone.”

“Girl Guide’s honour,” said Penny.

“You were in the Girl Guides?”

“No. I went to tap dancing lessons instead but there’s no such thing as tap dancer’s honour.”

“The story as she told it was that the football team were coming down from the college to the town. No idea why they weren’t with their teacher. Anyway, Frank Mountjoy was driving them in his little old car with a friend, Derek someone, and had come to something of an impasse with a bin lorry coming the other way. Blocked the entire road and path. Rather than back up and concede way to the bin lorry, Frank told the lads they could walk to the town just as quickly by going through a gate and over the meadow bit.”

"The mere."

"That's it. So, yes, when they did go wandering through and started to drown, Frank was there to help them out but..."

"He was sort of responsible for it in the first place."

Oscar's grin was impish now, almost devilish. Any nervousness had gone.

"But everyone wants to be the hero of their own story," he said.

# 24

When Izzy got to the shop on Friday morning, Aubrey was waiting outside.

"Come to paint our lobster?" she said.

He nodded his head energetically. "Paint a lobster, then paint a house. All in a day's work."

Only then did Izzy realise the shop door was still locked. Monty was on the other side, mouth open, tongue lolling, his breath making a misty circle on the glass.

"Penny not let you in?" she said as she unlocked.

Monty did capering circles around them as they entered.

"Penny!" Izzy called and wondered if — gosh! — she had spent the night somewhere else.

"Coming, coming," said Penny, noisily descending the stairs. Penny emerged into the shop with her top in a skewwhiff corkscrew around her waist.

She looked blearily at Aubrey.

"Are the paints here?" she asked.

"On the way," said Izzy, as she checked her phone. "Definitely here this morning it says."

Penny groaned and stared at the ceiling.

"Bad night?" suggested Aubrey.

"Or very good night," suggested Izzy.

Penny smacked dry lips. "Is there a thing where free wine gets you drunk quicker?"

"I think free wine gets drunk quicker generally," said Izzy. "How drunk you get is still down to you."

Penny, hungover, tried to focus on her own phone. "Fliss is coming round in an hour! If we can't start on the lobster right now, we've lost this commission. She won't want it if she can't have it for the car show."

Izzy went back into the tracking app. "I can see the delivery person is in the town. Maybe I can go and get to them early?"

Penny looked aghast. "You plan to go and accost the delivery driver at a different stop and persuade them to hand over a parcel?"

"Yes?" Izzy was confused. Why was Penny making it sound bad? "I'll hop on my bike and see where they are on the tracker."

"You do realise that you'll be like a highwayman, skidding in front of their van on your mad bike? I don't know whether you'll give them a heart attack or have them calling the police!" Penny said.

"A moment ago you were fretting about getting this paint in time. I am trying to fix things!" Izzy said.

"Is it Parv, the delivery guy?" asked Aubrey.

"The name of the delivery person is —" Izzy consulted

her phone "—Parv. How did you know that?"

Aubrey shrugged. "He's the local driver for the cheap courier."

"You assume we use the cheap courier," said Penny.

"I mean for small parcels, like when people buy things off eBay. I'll give him a call," said Aubrey.

"I don't think I can handle this," said Penny. "I need a coffee."

Izzy made a big inclusive gesture. "You could go get us all a coffee, couldn't you? Take Monty for a walk at the same time."

Penny squinted at the already sunny day. "Go outside?"

"Fresh air will do you the world of good."

Groaning like a reluctant zombie, Penny put a lead on Monty and took him out.

Within five minutes of Penny's departure, Aubrey had managed to get Parv on the phone and, five further minutes later, was out in front of the shop, fist bumping the courier as he jumped out of his van. Izzy signed for the package and they went inside to unwrap it.

Penny came back with three steaming coffees in a cardboard carrier, to find Izzy and Aubrey upstairs inspecting the paint colours.

"They aren't quite the same as I've used," said Aubrey, "but I think I can mix them up to make it work. Have you got something like a plastic lid I can use for mixing?"

"Um, let me think," said Penny who, despite having had some fresh air, didn't look like she was ready to do much thinking.

Izzy picked up a plastic pot of pins from the counter and

pulled off the lid. She tipped the pins into a pile and gave Aubrey the pot and its lid. "Go! Go!"

"Have we got time to do a practice one on the mock-up?" asked Aubrey.

A practice painting on the toile would have been ideal but Penny and Izzy both shook their heads.

"No time," said Penny.

"You can do this," said Izzy.

Izzy went to the mannequin and removed the overall. "I'll lay it out and put some plastic inside so that we don't transfer the paint to any other parts of the garment. You mix the paints. Penny, find a hairdryer."

Penny looked confused. "Why do we— oh. Yes."

Izzy laid out the overall and smoothed it flat. She inserted some strong plastic inside. Then she took another large piece of the plastic, cut a window into it, and placed it over the overall, so that the entire thing was protected, apart from where the lobster would be painted.

"Hey, I have prepared your patient!" she called.

"Huh. You really have!" Aubrey had mixed up the paints to recreate the colours he had used previously. "Do you have some scraps of this stuff, so I can see how it goes on?"

Izzy scrambled down the stairs and upended the scraps bucket. She found some of the white linen and ran back up with it. "Here!"

Aubrey applied his brush to the linen, dragging it across to emulate the curve of the lobster. "Oh man, this is really quite different."

"Do a couple more of those practice strokes, you'll be fine," said Izzy.

Aubrey shook his head. “I need to mix some more colour. It’s going to take more than I thought.”

Izzy nodded and made supportive noises.

Penny appeared in the doorway with the hairdryer, and then froze as they heard the shop door open.

“What if that’s Fliss?” she said.

“Just keep cool. She’s a customer. Go. Oh, take this.”

Penny flinched as Izzy threw her a hair scrunchy. Penny just stared at it.

“Tie your hair back. You look like you’ve been dragged through hedge backwards,” said Izzy. “Keep Fliss talking. Make her a drink. It will be fine.” Izzy was not known for being the voice of reason, but here, in the eye of the storm, she felt a serene confidence. It would all work out.

Penny trotted downstairs and Izzy could hear her greeting Fliss with a level of bright enthusiasm she had magically summoned from within.

Izzy turned back to Aubrey just in time to see a huge blog of paint fall from his tiny mixing palette onto the exposed window of the garment. They both stared in horror for a long moment. Izzy reached out a hand to rub it away, but Aubrey gave a panicked hiss and she stopped herself.

“A spoon or something?” he croaked.

Izzy fetched a spoon and Aubrey leaned over and scooped with the delicate precision of a surgeon, removing the excess.

He straightened and they both regarded the orange streak that remained.

“Well, if the lobster leaned the other way, it could work,”

said Izzy, holding up the paper version that Aubrey had done earlier, trying to illustrate what she meant.

"You're right. This can work. I think." Aubrey inhaled deeply and then set to work. Izzy tried to stay completely silent. She moved nothing apart from her eyes, watching Aubrey convert the accidental streak into a lobster, and listening to the small sounds of Penny being a charming host to Fliss downstairs. It was a few short minutes, but it felt like a lifetime before Aubrey finally straightened. "I think that's it," he declared.

Izzy plugged in the hairdryer and checked the settings. "Not too hot, it would be bad to melt the plastic or burn the paint." She set it on gentle heat and power, and wafted it at the design as Aubrey removed the surrounding plastic window. They both sat in silence with the noise of the hairdryer whining, as they watched the paint, trying to tell when it was dry enough.

"Try it now?" suggested Izzy.

Aubrey patted an edge with a finger. There was no transfer of paint. He patted in a few more places. "Looking good. I will remove the plastic from inside, so we can fan it around a bit."

Izzy held the overall leg clear as Aubrey pulled the plastic out, and Izzy blew air in with the hairdryer to keep the layers separate. She did that for a few more minutes. Could she hear a slightly anxious turn in the conversation downstairs? Penny was struggling to delay Fliss further, but they were nearly done now.

"Oh, no! I think we're supposed to heat set the paint!" she said, still wafting and drying. "What do the instructions say?"

Aubrey picked up one of the paints. "If you plan to wash the garment then you must iron on a low setting to set the paint in place."

"Oh, Penny!" Izzy shouted. "I'm just giving the overall a final press!"

She plugged in the iron and grabbed a towel to put below the lobster image. It took a few moments to arrange it so that it was positioned properly. She covered it with a pressing cloth made of silk organza and picked up the iron. She dabbed it onto the edge of the image.

"Will it stick to the cloth?" asked Aubrey.

Izzy lifted the cloth to demonstrate that it hadn't. It was time to go for it. She pressed it all over the image. She then used the iron to smooth some of the wrinkles they'd created as they manipulated it.

"Showtime!" she said to Aubrey, and they both went down to meet Penny and Fliss.

# 25

"Oh, there you are!" said Penny. Relief was rolling off her in waves.

Fliss looked impatient, her mouth set in a line, but her face softened when she saw that Izzy was carrying her garment. "Oh, let me see!"

Izzy held it up so that Fliss could take a look, but Fliss twitched it out of her hands.

"Oh, yes. Lovely."

"Isn't it?" said Izzy.

"How you managed it in time is beyond me. You're like the elves and the shoemaker. Except with dresses, of course."

"Of course," said Izzy.

"I'll put it on. I'm meeting the girls for morning drinks, so there's no time to lose. Will was supposed to drive me in this morning but he was too keen to get his car in a prime spot for the show weekend and left me *senza trasporto*."

Fliss disappeared to get changed.

"Right, I really need to go," said Aubrey. "Mr Dinktrout will have my guts for garters if I don't get that house front finished."

Aubrey's main employer was not only the owner of the big garden centre on the Badingham Road, but also the chair of the local chamber of commerce. Stuart Dinktrout was, Izzy knew, a demanding man and Aubrey needed to stay on the right side of him.

"You were wonderful," said Izzy.

"A magical elf indeed," added Penny. "I clearly owe you several pints now."

"Maybe you should let your head clear first," he grinned and slipped out of the shop.

"I don't think I did a good job of stalling her," said Penny. "I thought she was about to walk out. She's in a bit of a mood about Will coming into town without her."

"These car owners," said Izzy. "They all want their car in the best spot for the weekend show."

"It doesn't even start properly until tomorrow, does it?"

"No, but today's just as important for the real obsessives. It's all about the jostling and positioning and the pre-fun fun."

Fliss returned, squeaking with delight as she swooshed the flared trousers with a couple of small kicks.

She approached the mirror. "It feels like a million dollars, how does it look?" She twirled from side to side and inspected herself from every angle. "This is an absolute triumph. The giant trousers feel amazing. I wasn't sure if they might be too much, but they skim the floor and make me look like a goddess. As for the rest of it, it's exquisite! The top is so flattering and the lobster! How did you do it? It's a work of art, an actual work of art, and I get to wear it!" She grinned at them both. "I have never loved an outfit more than this!"

"We're so glad," said Izzy.

Fliss went over to her purse. "Now, you must need paying."

"That'd be nice," said Penny. It was perhaps meant to be a meaningless comment but, with the hangover, it sounded a little surly.

"Let's deal with that swiftly so you can be on your way," said Izzy and went to the counter.

Fliss took out several bank and credit cards and placed them on the counter. "Right, now I can't remember which ones Will said I wasn't to use. End of the month and all that."

The first card Izzy was given was declined. The second had insufficient funds on it. Eventually, a combination of three cards covered the cost of the dress and, with that sorted, Fliss Starling sailed out with a cheery wave.

"One happy customer," said Penny, wrapping her hands around her take-out coffee cup as if hugging it.

"Late night?" suggested Izzy gently.

"Not too late."

"Oh? Young Oscar didn't fit the bill?"

Penny blinked and stared, thoughtfully evaluating. "No. It was a good night."

Izzy gave her a sly look and pointed at the ceiling. "He's not still up there, is he?"

"Still?" said Penny.

"He is?"

"He is not!" she said. "We had a perfectly lovely evening. He's a fine conversationalist when he's loosened up. But, no, he caught a taxi back to his hotel once he'd walked me home."

Izzy gave her a penetrating look, hoping to elicit further details, but nothing more was forthcoming. Penny gave a big yawn.

"I can see you're going to be no use today," said Izzy.

"Sorry," Penny mumbled and sipped at her cup.

"My plans," said Izzy, "are to take young Monty here for a good long walk to tire him out and then sort out a parasol window display to draw visitors."

"My plans are..." Penny frowned.

"I'd like you to stay there, prop the counter up, drink caffeine and maybe later on tell me every detail of your date with Oscar."

"I think I can do that," said Penny. "Are you sure you're all right walking Monty? He's not your responsibility."

Izzy straightened. "I like taking him for walks. I thought maybe we ought to take him to Saxtead Grange. See if anyone actually wants this dog back."

"His owner is dead."

"Maybe someone else is going to inherit it."

"I don't think people put dogs in wills."

"People make all manner of funny requests when they die."

Izzy put on Monty's lead. He now had several, and Izzy had plans to make him some matching coats for inclement weather if he stayed with them.

"Besides, we can see if Monty has a good nose," she said. "If I'm not back in a couple of hours it's because he caught a whiff of sausages from the farm shop and dragged me across the fields to find them!"

# 26

The preparations for the car weekend were truly underway as Izzy walked through town. Spaces in the marketplace and along the major side roads were filling up with vehicles. The plan was to have most of the cars in the field beside the castle where there would also be a marquee, stalls and entertainment, but the event deliberately included cars dotted about the town centre for people to enjoy as they walked about.

As she set out with Monty, Izzy noticed that Will Starling's green Derby Bentley was already parked up in a prime spot in front of the Crown Hotel. Other cars were parked nearby. They ranged across makes, models and decades, from a maroon Sunbeam-Talbot, to a grey Morris Minor, to a pristine Ford Anglia painted blue like the car in Harry Potter. Proud owners loitered near their own cars or inspected each other's.

Monty led Izzy down the hill and through quieter roads to a footpath across fields.

"Know where you're going, huh?" she said.

Monty sniffed happily at the long luscious grass as they went. He had such short legs that the grass towered over him, and he had to nose his way in where the smell needed further investigation.

"We should get you some stilts, Monty. Or a little jetpack!"

As they pottered along the path, Izzy tried to work out where they were by peering over the hedgerow onto the road, but it was just a little bit too tall.

"I also need a jetpack."

There was a gap in the hedge a little further along, and a stile to climb over.

"Ah, interesting. How are you with stiles?"

Izzy approached the stile, wondering if she'd have to carry Monty over, but as they came close to it, he hopped through a dog-sized gap at the base.

"Very good. You've done this before."

Izzy threaded the lead through the gap and climbed over. There was a further path cut through the crop, which were handsome knee-high plants with black and white flowers. Some had small pods developing, which Izzy thought might be peas or beans. She looked all around to check that she wasn't being observed and picked one off a plant and opened it. She popped the tiny broad beans inside into her mouth, their sweetness added to by the thrill of having committed an admittedly very minor theft.

Monty made an excited huffing sound and yanked hard to the left.

"Wha—?"

Izzy barely had time to react as he tore off along the hedgerow. There was a gap between the hedge and the crops, but it teetered on the edge of a deep ditch. There was movement up ahead and Izzy realised that Monty had caught sight of a hare. It must be a hare as it was enormous compared to the rabbits that Izzy was more accustomed to. She had seen them in the petting zoo and they were little fluffballs that you could cup in your hands. This thing was huge and feral and looked at them both with eyes that betrayed no fear. It loped down into the ditch and disappeared from view. Monty was in a frenzy. Not only had the exciting thing moved, it had initiated a game of hide-and-seek!

He yanked on the lead and sent Izzy tumbling down the bank into the ditch. There was water in the bottom of the ditch, of course there was. Izzy's arm and shoulder plunged into it, and the rest of her stalled as the collar of her shirt was caught on something. She found herself suspended in a really uncomfortable position. Her throat was constricted by her collar. Her legs...where were her legs? They were flailing somewhere uselessly above her, failing to get a grip on the slope of the ditch. One of her arms was in the frigid water of the ditch, and her other arm still held the straining lead of Monty.

"Monty!" she called in a strangled voice. This was the time for him to shine like a wonder-dog. He could help her by using some sort of doggie leverage to drag her back up the bank. Maybe she should have the faith to let go of the lead so that he could fetch help?

No. What he was actually doing was yipping and straining in fury because he couldn't get to the hare, which was presumably long gone. He was pulling at her arm in such a frenzy that the most likely outcome was her fully faceplanting into the ditch if he dragged her free of whatever it was she was caught up on.

She had no sense of what to adjust to make her situation better; indeed it felt very much as if all of the available options would result in making things worse. She moved her legs, searching for any purchase. Her left foot found something solid and she used the leverage to pull back on Monty's lead. She needed that hand!

The lead loosened, and Monty came back around to see what she was doing. Izzy found herself hoping that *now* was the time for the appearance of wonder-dog. She waited for him to at least nuzzle her face to make her feel better, but instead Monty rushed at her and yipped in excitement, bounding onto her back and jumping between her shoulderblades.

He seemed to think that accelerating the choking of his human was a game. This was not good news. Izzy's throat was really quite uncomfortable, although she found some pride in having sewn that top button securely onto her blouse. She had no idea that it could withstand such force.

The button popped off and Izzy splashed down face first into the water. She pushed up out of it.

"Blah!" she exclaimed, surfacing.

But at least she was able to move now. She scrabbled

through what felt like a good many tiny manoeuvres to try to avoid getting her entire body soaked in ditch water, but gravity was against her and Monty jumped joyfully back and forth as her feet finally found the bottom and she pushed out against it, scrabbling up the muddy sides. Part of her brain wanted to find the missing button, but she pushed it angrily aside.

As she finally stood on the side of the ditch and rose on shaky legs, she spotted the remains of her blouse's collar ripped off on a stumpy thorn branch. She didn't need to feel her neck to know that it was red with the pressure of having been all but strangled by her own clothes. She was cold and utterly filthy.

"Well thanks, Monty. I see you missed the wonder-dog training. At least you won't have to look too far to find something interesting to smell."

Monty gave a small bark of approval. It seemed that ditch water was his favourite perfume.

Izzy wanted to sulk and return immediately in search of sympathy and cleanliness, but the sun warmed her as she retraced her steps to the footpath.

"We'll press on, Monty. We've come this far, let's take a look."

They turned onto the footpath and walked into the field away from the ditch.

Izzy was glad that she was wearing boots, even soggy ones, as the surface of the field was ridged and uneven from its ploughing earlier in the season. Monty trotted through what must have been quite a daunting tunnel for a dog of his stature, but he tugged with some force, so the smells in the field were obviously to his liking.

The sky was cloudless and blue overhead, and after a few minutes, Izzy was surrounded by broad bean plants on every side. Her world was currently like a very simple painting, saturated with bright blue and the strange grey-green of the plants. If she ignored the cold sogginess and the weird smell, it was almost idyllic.

As she reached the top of the slope she could see a shape further along in the field. It looked like someone just standing there. Simply standing. Were they performing some sort of sun salutation? Was she intruding on a private ritual?

Every step took her a little closer, and Monty was pulling more and more enthusiastically, so she was able to make out more detail. Whoever it was, they were wearing a hat. Izzy thought that was sensible, as the sun was quite bright. She should probably have worn one herself. She glanced down at Monty. A hat for Monty would be a marvellous thing to make! Her mind immediately reached for possible designs. What sort of a hat would suite him best? There was a border collie called Star who sometimes featured in the Frambeat Gazette wearing a beret. Monty's ears were surely too perky to accommodate a beret?

Monty yipped briefly. Izzy was surprised, and wondered if it was in answer to her thoughts about berets, but she quickly realised that Monty was not telepathic but was instead highly focused on the path. Was he reacting to the person up ahead? They were still motionless, which was weird.

"Oh wait. It's only weird if you're a real person and not a scarecrow!" Izzy declared, mostly to the scarecrow itself.

Izzy laughed out loud at her mistake. As to why Monty wanted to reach it so badly, it was a puzzle, but perhaps he just really liked scarecrows.

It was a few minutes later that they reached the scarecrow, and Izzy felt foolish for thinking it was a person, because she wasn't sure it was even fooling the crows. It was supported by a long pole that ran up its trouser leg and through the back of its jacket. Its head was made from an upside-down plastic container, the sort of thing that would hold a gallon of screenwash for a car. The open top was duct-taped onto the wooden pole and there was a rudimentary face drawn onto it. Straw had been draped over the container head to give it a mop of brittle blond hair.

Izzy discovered that the scarecrow had been given form from bin bags stuffed with straw, because she could see it emerging at the edges where it had been ravaged by the weather (and perhaps the crows, if they had been trying to make a point). Oddly, though, it wore a cap and a jacket that looked in much better condition than the rest of it. Both were made from good quality tweed. The blue cap was in the baker boy style, although she found that she wanted to call it a driving cap. It gave the scarecrow a casual look, as if he had paused halfway across the field to tip his cap back and gaze at something interesting. Izzy turned to see where he was looking and found that she could see Saxtead Grange in the distance.

"Interesting."

She turned back to look at the jacket. Again, it wasn't

worn out. It was strange that this scarecrow was so well-dressed. It was tempting to take it, as she was experiencing a damp wardrobe crisis of her own. She dithered. She ummed and she ahhed. And then a momentary breeze blew over and she shivered from her neck to her wet tummy.

"Sorry, Sir. I need this more than you do," she said and awkwardly relieved the scarecrow of his jacket.

She put it on and, even though it was oversized and pressed her wet blouse against her body, she felt immediately better.

Monty was impressed too, as he stood on his back legs and pawed at her. He then dropped back down and plunged into the broad beans.

"No, wait! We can't walk there. We need to stick to the path!"

Monty was heedless of the country code and battled to drag Izzy into the crops. For such a small dog he could muster some power when he wanted to. Izzy gazed at the path that he apparently wanted to take and saw that there were already a lot of broken and flattened plants.

"What is it boy? What can you smell, Monty?"

Feeling slightly ridiculous, Izzy sniffed the air, just in case she too could sense whatever it was Monty could smell over the more obvious stench of ditch water. She bent down and sniffed the ground and then she sniffed the scarecrow for good measure. She thought she had a whiff of something from the jacket, but it was very fleeting and she couldn't put a name to it.

It was very clear that Monty wanted to follow the trampled crops. Given the path evidently led in the direction of Saxtead Grange, it seemed like too much of a coincidence to ignore.

"All right, but don't squash any more of these poor plants. The farmer will be furious!"

She trod carefully, examining the ground for clues, footprints and a path around the plants, although Monty had no problem taking the most direct route.

Izzy tried to work out whether she could tell anything about who or what might have made this path. Could it have been a deer or a badger? She had a feeling that only a human would have stomped a path quite so messily. It was not possibly to tell whether it was a big human or a small one, as there were no footprints at all that she could find. She wondered if the Clown Menace could be behind this, but there was nothing obvious like a discarded mask.

As they drew nearer to the grounds of Saxtead Grange, Izzy looked around to see whether the trail led to the left or the right. The answer turned out to be neither. The hedge that separated the field from the garden had a hole. It wasn't the usual thick, thorny type of hedge, but was made from some sort of ornamental evergreen and someone had simply kicked their way through it, leaving a tight but passable route through into the grounds.

Izzy might have hesitated, but Monty wanted to get through and take a look at his former home. Izzy followed because, if nothing else, it would mean she could find her way back to the road more easily.

As long as she didn't bump into an angry farmer who had given his best jacket to a scarecrow, she would be fine.

# 27

She emerged through the gap in the hedge into the large garden that surrounded Saxtead Grange. The large fish pond (or was that small fishing lake?) was off to her right, and the outbuildings containing the car garages were to her left. Straight ahead was the main house itself. Up high, a bedroom window was open and a curtain fluttered in the breeze.

"So, this is the way you escaped, is it, Monty?" Izzy said, and she realised she was whispering, as if trespass had brought out the furtive nature in her. "We'll go back via the road, eh?"

She took a step to the right and then stopped. A woman came out of the house and crossed the lawn to a long sagging clothes line with a big basket of washing in her hands. It was the servant woman, or maid or house drudgeon or whatever they called her. Susie or Sarah or something.

Izzy wasn't sure why she had stopped in order to avoid

being noticed. Was she really trespassing? Technically, yes, obviously. But she had Monty with her and surely Monty still sort of belonged to this house. She was just giving the boy a walk around his own estate.

Besides, Monty was pulling in the opposite direction, round to the left, towards the outbuildings.

"Okay, just a little walk," she said.

She suspected the little hound still had a fondness for this place. She revised this opinion when she saw he was heading straight for a low bucket of kitchen scraps by a door. It was low enough that he could get his paws on the lip and his head inside, like a fuzzy piggy at a trough. Someone had broken up and thrown away a dozen misshapen scotch eggs and Monty guzzled at them greedily.

"I'm sure they'll give you wind," she said.

The wall beside her held the doors to the garages. They were shut although she supposed Frank's car, like Will's, was gone, parked in a suitably prominent position in town for the car weekend. Would the dead Derek's car still be in there? There was another door nearer to Izzy and, while Monty continued to snuffle and chomp, Izzy stepped closer and peered through the gap in the dark wood.

The gleam and shape of metal within drew her interest and, when Monty had wolfed down his sixth or seventh egg, she pulled the bolt open and looked inside.

It was another garage space. There were plenty more tools and a modern workbench, and on the floor in the middle was a car. Well, it was sort of a car. It was like one of those exploded diagrams that showed you how to put your flat pack wardrobe together, although this wasn't a wardrobe, it was a very old car. There were spindles and rods and nuts and bolts and linkages, all of them laid out on the clean floor. Burgundy outer body panels rested against the walls, and Izzy could see that many of them were savagely bent and completely out of shape.

"Oh."

She suddenly realised what the was looking at, and felt as if she was walking over someone's grave.

"Can I help you?" said a voice.

A broad, older woman in jeans and a cream jumper was in the yard behind her.

"Oh, I am sorry," said Izzy and pointed at the dog. "Monty here was irresistibly drawn by the kitchen scraps."

The woman looked at the dog.

"Dog walker?"

"Dressmaker, actually," said Izzy. "It's a rather complicated story." She gestured at the door and the half-built wreck of the red car within. "I'm sorry. I was curious."

The woman stepped a little closer so she could see the car too.

"It's all right. Will keeps tinkering with it. His own car is the Derby Bentley with the sports saloon body. My Monty's was the Thrupp and Maberly coupe de ville body. Much more elegant, I thought."

Izzy realised who the woman was.

"I'm Izzy King," she said.

"Jacqui Bildeston," said the woman and frowned at Izzy's clothes. "You appear to be damp."

"Monty pulled me into a ditch."

Jacqui grunted in strange satisfaction. "Yes, Monty. I've

never had time for dogs. Too needy. Like children and husbands. Do you want to come in for a cup of tea and I'll get Susan to dry it for you?"

"That's very kind."

"By the way, I love your skirt. That Laura Ashley pattern has always been my favourite."

"Thank you," said Izzy and swished her skirts obligingly as she followed the woman inside.

# 28

The kitchen at Saxtead Grange was a huge affair, with a giant aga at one end in front of a huge breasted chimney that Izzy thought must surely be original to the old house. At the other end were all the trappings and furniture of a traditional farmhouse kitchen large enough to seat the farmer and eleven of his farmhands if he so wished. Jacqui Bildeston, widow of the original Monty Bildeston, found Izzy a T-shirt to wear and, without any social embarrassment, told Izzy to take off her blouse.

"Not sure the jacket is your size," said Jacqui, looking at it curiously.

"I found it," said Izzy. "On a scarecrow."

"Ah. I can get rid of it if you like," she said and made to take.

"I might need the warmth for the walk home," said Izzy.

Jacqui turned to call out through the kitchen door. "Susan, can you get this dry?"

The servant woman came in and took the blouse from her. "I've just had to put the laundry in the dryer. Bloody masked pranksters have stolen my line prop, haven't they?"

Izzy wasn't sure if Susan threw an accusatory glance at her before she left. Jacqui poured a pot of tea and searched cupboards for biscuits or cakes.

"I was enjoying having the house to myself this morning," she said.

"Sorry for intruding."

Jacqui's smile flickered. "Or rather, I was enjoying having certain people out of the house. The Starlings and the Mountjoys are in town, meeting some others for lunch. You know the Starlings and the Mountjoys?"

"Increasingly so," said Izzy. "Fliss bought an outfit from us. Carmella has a, er, similar shop to us in Wickham Market."

Jacqui made an amused noise. "Over-priced clothes for stick thin women."

Izzy said nothing. It was true that alongside 'stick thin' Carmella and long, elegant Fliss, Jacqui was robustly built.

"You know how hard it is to find clothes to fit me?" asked Jacqui.

"I make my own," said Izzy. "It's how I got started in sewing, really. I'm sorry to hear about your friend, Derek, by the way."

Jacqui located a jug of milk, brought it over to the table and put down a thickly glazed terracotta teapot on a raffia mat.

"Sad in its own way," she said, which struck Izzy as a

peculiar phrase. "After my Monty and his Gertie were killed, there was always this thing between us, a horrible unspoken bond. We could never be normal people with each other again. It was as if we were handcuffed together. As if we had joint custody of a tragedy." She frowned at herself and then dismissed the thoughts, waving them away like flies.

"Well, I hope the police find the person who did it."

"I'm sure everyone gets their just desserts in the end," said Jacqui with firm conviction. She took off the teapot lid, prodded the tea bags with a spoon, and deciding that the pot had brewed enough, poured. "Death comes suddenly, doesn't it?"

"I really wouldn't know," said Izzy.

"One moment you're there and then — plop! — darkness takes you."

"I suppose."

"I was quite short with Derek the night before he died," said Jacqui.

"I can imagine he could be irritating."

"It was questions, questions, questions over dinner. The very last words I ever spoke to him were to tell him to leave me alone. That was it. Last words."

Izzy put a splash of milk in her tea.

"You hear anything that morning?" said Izzy. "I mean, when Derek was attacked."

Jacqui shook her head. "I think I was some distance away. I hadn't had a great night's sleep. Will was shouting at the dog around midnight because the excitable thing was scratching at the doors downstairs. I assume he was shouting at the dog. Something incomprehensible and then "I'll bloody kill him." Bit harsh. I never sleep well here. Not since… I only come because it's expected, but really I need my own bed."

"I love strange beds," said Izzy.

"Is that so?"

Izzy twitched her lips. "Having said that, I fear it sounds as if I like jumping into strangers' beds. I mean I like sleeping different places. No, that doesn't sound much better."

"I like my own bed," reiterated Jacqui. "I got up early that morning. I met Carmella on the stairs, both of us in dressing gowns and slippers. The dog was playing out in the yard. I remember that. We came down here and, perhaps because she'd not slept so well either, Carmella was in fractious mood."

Izzy smiled but said nothing.

"She had decided to tell me that no one liked the scotch eggs I made for our traditional picnic. That they were too greasy and made everything else smell."

Izzy might have pointed out that Monty the dog clearly liked them but suspected that would not help.

"Words were said in this very kitchen," said Jacqui, "and I decided I would need to take a walk or I would end up saying things to Carmella Mountjoy that one of us would later regret. She strode off serenely to enjoy her tea on the lawns and I went for a very angry walk in the fields."

"Going for a walk is a good way to alleviate a bad mood," Izzy agreed.

"Yes, although I might have taken my frustrations out physically on a scarecrow."

"I'm sure he's used to it."

"I came back to find my scotch eggs in the bin and Frank yelling about Derek being dead. Perfectly ridiculous, all of it."

A short while later, Susan reappeared with a much dryer blouse, albeit one with a seriously damaged collar.

"I can't find it anywhere," she said, exasperated.

Izzy frowned at her.

"The big prop for the clothes line. It's got to be those hoodlums in the masks."

Jacqui gave Izzy a freshly quizzical look. "Is yours the shop that's been selling all those masks to underage criminals?"

"Not selling," said Izzy. "And I don't think they're all criminals."

Jacqui nodded without comment.

Once Izzy was changed, Jacqui walked her out into the courtyard. Monty the dog sniffed round the scraps bucket near the open door to the garage.

"Betrayal hurts," said Jacqui. "People do things thinking you'll never find out or not thinking anything at all."

Izzy wasn't sure whether she was talking about binned scotch eggs or Monty and Gertie's final fatal affair, if affair it was.

"People can be thoughtless," Izzy agreed politely. She waggled Monty's lead. "You know this really isn't my dog."

"I know."

"I don't know if someone wants it back."

"Can't imagine anyone does," said Jacqui. "I know Derek thought he meant well in naming the pooch, but I can't stand hearing Monty's name used like that. Best if you take him away."

"Understandable," said Izzy.

With a dry blouse and a borrowed jacket, Izzy walked down the gravel driveway to the track that would lead them back to town.

# 29

On her return to town, Izzy found evidence of Tariq's investigations into the masked miscreant menace. He'd posted on social media, following up every incident of alleged pranking, theft or vandalism carried out by little people wearing end-of-line masks from Cozy Craft. Now, she saw, he had gone beyond social media and had put posters on several of the lampposts.

*Have you been a victim of the masked menace?*

The posters included Tariq's contact details so that people could share details, but Izzy wondered if they also might be responsible for an escalation, both in the number of incidents and people's reactions to them.

Indeed, on the noticeboard outside the library, Izzy could see that new flyers had appeared beneath Tariq's. One was offering paid counselling services to those affected by masked-inflicted trauma. Another offered legal assistance to those who wanted to pursue the menaces for damages to their well-being or their businesses.

"Penny, the mask hysteria is growing," she called as she went back into the shop.

Penny looked up from her coffee, possibly her third of the morning.

"Whut? Um, where did you get that jacket from?"

"Borrowed it off a scarecrow for genuine reasons," Izzy said. "But I promised to return it."

"It's quite nice."

"I thought so too. Clearly, we get a better class of scarecrow round here."

Izzy had already produced a good collection of parasols. She had been pleased with the ones that she had made from the leftover linen from the lobster overall, but since then she had branched out and experimented with some broderie anglaise fabric. With its fluttering, delicate designs worked in white thread on a white background, the result was perfect. Then she decided to use more colour, so she made one from blue chambray. Penny had been puzzled by the chambray because of its superficial resemblance to denim. It wasn't until she felt how much lighter it was that she understood how it could be used for a parasol. It gave Izzy an idea though, and she finished it with some piping and some fringing around the edges, so that it had a rodeo aesthetic.

She spent some time filling the window with out-turned parasols, checking from the street to see that the display was as impactful as she thought it might be, and was pleased with the results.

When that was done, she showed Penny one of Tariq's inflammatory flyers.

"Check these out."

Penny scanned the piece of paper. "I've heard some of the other shops have been suffering from petty thefts and minor acts of vandalism. Apparently, a small Elton John stole some eggs and threw them at the hardware store earlier," said Penny.

"Isn't Elton John quite small anyway?" asked Izzy. "And either rumours are spreading or we've got a crimewave on our hands. The maid woman up at Saxtead Grange said they'd come and stolen her line prop."

"Isn't that a rugby position?"

"Line prop, as in a big stick to hold up her washing line."

"And we're getting the blame?"

"It's possible."

Penny looked queasy, although Izzy wasn't sure if that might be the remnants of the hangover "No! Surely not? We can't have that. Whatever will people think? Especially now there's been a murder, too. Feelings are running high. Our reputation could be dragged right down if we're blamed for this."

Izzy shrugged. "There's probably not much we can do about it."

Penny nodded. "You're right." She pulled a pained expression.

Izzy was happy with the window now, and as she straightened as an idea came to her. "I think I'll just take five and pop over to the Co-op for a chocolate bar. Want anything?"

"I've got a Kit Kat multipack if you want one?" said Penny.

"No thank you, I fancy something different, see you in a bit."

Izzy went over to the shop and swiftly made her purchases, then walked slowly back towards the shop. It was important to make sure there was nobody directly watching, so she took her time. Her hand slipped into her bag and closed around one of the eggs in the box she had just bought. She swung her arm down by her side, the movement completely natural, except for the egg that was concealed in her palm.

She looked around and saw that the other pedestrians were all either facing away or staring at their phones. She whipped her arm back and flung the egg at the window of Cozy Craft.

"Oh no! Come back here, you hooligan!" she shouted at a distant spot where the imaginary assailant had run off to.

"Izzy, are you all right?" Penny ran outside and stared at Izzy and then at the egg running down the frontage.

"We'd best get a picture of that before we clean it off," said Izzy. "Should wipe off easily enough while it's fresh, but maybe you want to post it on social media? I mean, at least it shows that we've been targeted as well, so we're probably not involved in the attacks."

Penny ran a little further out and looked frantically from side to side. "But did you see them? Who did this?"

"Oh, you know me, Penny, I was in a world of my own. I'm really not sure. I'll get a bucket and a cloth, shall I?"

# 30

With the roads closed and the car show not properly underway, Friday business was a little slow. An afternoon of hot drinks and comforting biscuits soon cured Penny of any lingering hangover. Nonetheless, it became an afternoon of quiet tasks, of sorting stock and tidying.

Izzy stooped to scratch Monty behind his ear. "Do you have a dog now, Penny?"

"Do I?"

"It looks like you have a dog."

"Maybe someone will come and claim him still?"

"Really?"

"I don't know," said Penny. "Why have *I* got a dog? Why haven't *you* got a dog?"

"You found him, didn't you?" said Izzy. "It's one of them finders keepers things."

"I don't think that is an actual legal thing."

"Reckon it is," said Izzy.

Monty rolled over to have his tummy scratched and Izzy obliged.

"Maybe you're right. *We* have a dog. The shop has a dog."

"I'm not a hundred percent sure dogs and sewing shops go together. Although, he's been no trouble at all, has he?" Penny said, ignoring the cake incident.

Izzy suddenly had an idea that pleased her on multiple levels.

"I'm going to make Monty a bed."

"He's got a box," said Penny.

"No. An actual bed."

Making him a bed was pleasing on a basic level because Monty would be comfortable and it wouldn't cost them any money. What added some extra zest was the idea that Izzy might use some of the materials from the recycling bin. Penny kept threatening to throw away the recycling if it overflowed the dustbin-sized container that held it, but Izzy wasn't sure she really meant it. Some of the fabric scraps went to schools for crafts, but it seemed as though they could create scraps faster than the schools could use them.

Izzy dipped in to find scraps of the sturdiest fabric. Mostly that meant calico, and some pieces of denim too. She looked for the largest pieces and piled them up beside the sewing machine.

"Know what I'm doing Monty, eh? I am doing some crazy patchwork." The dog did not look impressed. "Fine. Do you want to know why? I am making scraps into yardage so that I can make you a dog bed. A lovely scrappy dog bed, how would that be?"

"Are you talking to yourself or the dog?" asked Penny.

"You might be interested to know how to do this," said Izzy, waggling the rotary cutter at her. "Making scraps into yardage for a project."

Penny came over. "Reducing the scraps sounds great."

"Crazy patchwork is something the Victorians used to do by hand, but we can do it using the machine. We start in the middle and build outwards, sewing straight lines across the work to extend it with new pieces."

Izzy demonstrated for Penny, turning the work and making it a little larger every time.

"You're going to run out of pieces that are long enough to attach," said Penny.

Izzy threw her some pieces from the pile. "Good spot. Let's speed things up then, you can join those into strips and then I can use them. Trim them with the rotary cutter."

"The rotary cutter? I don't like it. I always think I'll cut myself, it's so sharp," said Penny.

"It's also the best way to get a straight edge. Just think of it as a pizza cutter for fabric. Use the acrylic ruler, keep your fingers clear and you'll be fine."

With the two of them working together, they had soon created the large pieces needed for the dog bed. Izzy assembled it into something that looked like a pillowcase.

"And now we stuff it!"

"What will we use?" asked Penny.

"More scraps! In an ideal world we'd be better at sorting the scraps. We use the cabbage for stuffing things."

Penny looked up from what she was doing. "It sounded like you just said we'd use cabbage for stuffing things."

"Yeah, that is what I said. Cabbage is the name for scraps that are too small to do any sewing with. Little trimmings." Izzy dropped some from her outstretched fingers to demonstrate.

"Oh yes! It does look a bit like sliced cabbage."

"It's a word with an interesting history. Nobody's certain, but it might not be named after the vegetable, but from the French word *cabasser* which meant to toss things into a basket."

"Another Word Nerd special! You know what that means then?" said Penny. "Your next scrap-busting project will be to sew a basket for the cabbage. You can even put a label on it with the embroidery machine."

"Aye aye, captain!" said Izzy, as she started pushing scraps into the dog bed.

Izzy knew that the comfiest bed would be one that was stuffed as firmly as possible, so all of the scraps made their way in before she sewed up the gap.

"Here you go Monty, what a fabulous bed this is! What do you think?"

She put it down by the counter and Monty approached it, gave it a brief sniff and hopped on, walking in circles before settling down for a snooze on his new crazy patchwork bed.

By the counter, Penny was inspecting the jacket Izzy had borrowed from the scarecrow.

"This is good quality, isn't it? Tell me again how you got this?"

"Why?"

"Because I don't think a mysterious masked miscreant killed Derek Masters."

# 31

Evening was settling over Framlingham. From the seats by the window of Penny's little room, she could see over the marketplace. At the close of day, Fram marketplace was often empty, the life and energy of the town retired for the night. Tonight, Market Hill was full of cars representing almost every decade of the past hundred years. The Crown Hotel was doing a roaring trade, with drinkers getting in on the weekend celebrations early. The little Indian restaurant in the square seemed absolutely full and there was even a queue at the door.

Izzy came up the stairs from the kitchenette with two tall mugs of hot chocolate. Monty came trotting up beside her.

"It's a warm evening so I put a scoop of vanilla ice cream in the top of them," she said.

"Interesting choice," said Penny.

Izzy put the drinks on the little table and dropped into

her armchair. Monty found a dark secluded spot under the table and flopped.

"Right, Izzy," said Penny, putting her mobile phone on the table. "Where was this scarecrow?"

Izzy looked at the map app on the screen. "Well, I reckon that if we walked up along the hedgerow here then it would be about.... Here. Yes, here."

Penny looked at where Izzy had tapped and zoomed out a little. "Well within sight of one side of Saxtead Grange."

"Oh, I see where you're going with this," said Izzy.

Penny sipped her hot chocolate and vanilla ice cream. It was definitely creamy and gave her a momentary vanilla moustache.

"Let's run through what happened at Saxtead Grange that night," she said. "Everyone was at dinner. Frank bored everyone with his 'I rescued a bunch of young footballers story' —"

"Which is a load of fibs really," said Izzy.

"And Derek knew it because he was there. And Derek was being irritating at dinner too, badgering Jacqui with questions of some sort which led her to loudly tell him to leave her alone. Then everyone goes to bed and all is quiet, apart from Will shouting at little Monty for scratching at the doors in the night."

"Correct."

"At best guess, Carmella and Jacqui are first up. They meet, they have an argument about the quality of Jacqui's scotch eggs and Jacqui goes out for a walk to calm herself while Carmella, ice queen that she is, takes tea on the lawn."

"At least Monty liked the scotch eggs," observed Izzy. "Frank wakes next, possibly disturbed by the dog barking in the yard. He gets up, looks out the window and sees a miscreant in a Boris Johnson mask, or so he thinks. He goes downstairs, is drawn to the garage by Monty's barking and finds Derek, dead."

"God rest his soul."

"God rest his soul. Frank starts shouting and yelling. Fliss and Will are the only ones still in bed. Fliss hears Frank, wakes up and then wakes Will and now everyone's called to the crime scene and the police are summoned."

"Correct," said Penny. "Everyone either has an alibi, or at the very least, their actions fit in with what everyone else is saying."

"Except you think the masked attacker Frank saw was actually the scarecrow. He saw it moving, though."

Penny nodded. "You said that Jacqui, while out walking, had taken out her frustrations on a scarecrow. Maybe punched it and knocked it around. Maybe she even uprooted it and put it back in the ground."

"Just as Frank was looking out the window," nodded Izzy. "A plastic tub head and a mop of straw hair might resemble old Bojo from a distance. That confirms both Jacqui's and Frank's stories, even if Frank was mistaken."

"But it means there was probably no masked attacker after all. These last few days, people have found it easier to blame bad things on naughty boys in masks than seek more obvious explanations."

"So, who killed Derek then?" said Izzy.

Penny shrugged. "If we ignore the idea of a random

intruder for now, then our list of suspects is limited to the five people in that house."

"*Our* list of suspects?"

"We have hot chocolate to drink and it's a fine mental exercise." She smiled wryly. "I also think that staging a fake egging on our shop is unlikely to stop people linking us to the masked crime wave, so we have our own reputation to save."

"Oh, you saw that."

"It was a clever idea though. Very Izzy."

"I will take that as a compliment. So our suspects. Do they all have a motive?"

"Jacqui," said Penny. "The consensus is that Derek's womanising behaviour possibly drove Gertie into Monty's arms —"

Under the table, Monty the dog made a querying grumble noise.

"Not you," said Penny. "— drove Gertie into Monty's arms and thus, in a roundabout way, was responsible for them being in a crash."

Izzy pulled an uncertain face. "We're all assuming — all of us — that Monty and Gertie were having an affair because they died in a crash together. In terms of Jacqui's motive for killing Derek, it seems more likely she'd just had enough of Derek's romantic advances. The one thing everyone agreed upon was that Derek was a pest that night at the dinner table."

"If we are to believe Carmella then Derek had also had an affair with Fliss some years back. It strikes me now that Will mentioned how generous Derek was to Fliss and Will's daughter Caroline when she got married. Affectionate, too. That was the word he used."

Izzy pulled back, surprised. "Caroline is Derek's child?"

"If Will knew it or Fliss wanted to keep it hidden, would that be motive enough to kill Derek, years after the event?"

"And what about Frank and Carmella?"

Penny thought on that. "Frank is a proud man who, amongst all his other boorish behaviour, has dined out on that drowning footballers story for years."

"But Derek knew that the truth casts Frank in a very different light."

"Worth killing a man for?" said Penny doubtfully.

"So, our motives. Jacqui wanted Derek dead to stop him harassing her and as payback for Monty's death."

Monty the dog whined.

"Not you, Monty," said Izzy. "Will wanted to kill him for fathering a child with his wife. And Fliss perhaps wanted to kill him to keep that hushed up. Similarly, Frank wanted him dead to protect his honour and his stupid little story. And Carmella?"

"Never had a nice thing to say about Derek."

"Never had a nice thing to say about anyone."

"And yet she strikes me as someone with an intense loyalty to her friends. Could she have killed Derek in support of those friends, for any of the reasons we've just been through? To protect Jacqui? To keep the past secret? Maybe to avenge the deaths of Gertie and Monty?"

Monty yipped.

"Not you, Monty!" the pair of them said as one.

And a thought struck Penny. Actually, it wasn't a thought.

There was a hole in her mind, an empty space where a thought should be, and Monty's yipping had opened it up or pointed out it was there, and Penny racked her mind to work out what it was. She closed her eyes and put her fingertips to her temple.

"Ice cream headache?" said Izzy.

Penny ignored her for a moment.

"The dog…" she said. "In the night time."

"Monty? Yes."

"Most people's accounts involve the dog, either barking or not barking or just being a pain."

"You're not a pain, are you?" said Izzy and tousled Monty's ears.

"In the night, Will shouted at the dog for scratching at the doors."

"Correct."

"Jacqui heard the dog outside when she was coming downstairs and met Carmella. When Carmella came into this shop, she said Monty had been out in the flower beds when she was taking early morning tea."

"She did."

"Frank said that Monty's barking outside woke him and that it was Monty's barking that enticed him over to the garage."

"Indeed."

"Fliss and Will didn't get up until after Derek's body had been found."

"Yes?"

Penny closed her eyes again and thought hard, checking over her thinking. "So who let Monty out? He was in, scratching at doors, and then he was out, but no one let him out."

Izzy blinked and then released a long "Oooh" of interest. "Good point. Although, that was probably Derek because he got up to go to the garage."

Penny tutted at herself. "Oh. I thought I had something there. Phooey."

"I mean we don't even know why he was in the garage. Just buffing up his car?" Izzy pulled a puzzled face. "But the thing about the dog..."

Izzy took out her phone and dialled a number. Penny gave her pointed questioning looks but Izzy ignored her.

"Ah. Hello," said Izzy. "Sorry to bother you so late. No. Oh. I'm really glad you like it. I've got a very random question to ask you. On Tuesday night, the night before — yes, that night. Did you hear Will shouting at the dog? In the night, I mean." Izzy nodded as the caller responded. "No, I know it's a very strange request. And we've got Monty here. Very settled he is. But I wondered if — Ah. Ah, okay. Oh, that's interesting. Thank you. Bye."

She put the phone down.

"Well, well, well," she said.

"Do tell," said Penny.

"Two curious things. One — that was Fliss by the way — Fliss says she did *not* hear Will shouting at the dog."

"But they share a room."

"And she said she was a light sleeper."

"So that doesn't work."

"She *says* she's a light sleeper," said Izzy. "Plenty of people bizarrely pride themselves on being light sleepers even when they're not."

"So she didn't hear Will shouting and...?"

"And what else didn't she hear in the night, hmmm? What if she didn't hear Will getting up early, going outside, letting Monty out in the process, and nipping off to kill Derek in the garage before coming back in and climbing back into bed?"

"Where Fliss would 'wake him' some time later to tell him that Derek was dead. Blimey, that is clever, Izzy."

"Isn't it? And Will murdered him as revenge for his affair with Fliss or to stop him harassing Jacqui or to get him to stop trying to be a dad to Caroline."

"Pick a motive, any motive," Penny conceded. She looked at her mug of chocolate. There was only a gloopy sludge of melted ice cream left in the bottom. She wondered if she could slurp it out and retain her dignity.

"Want to hear the other curious thing?" said Izzy.

"Yes?"

"Fliss hasn't seen Will all day today. He's not come home this evening. As far as she's concerned, he's gone missing."

"Oh, that is interesting," said Penny. "A murderer gone on the run?"

"Perhaps."

Penny looked at the ice cream sludge in her mug and decided she would go for it. She upended the mug to drink it down. It did not end well.

# 32

Penny had so many thoughts occupying her mind that she woke early on Saturday morning. Some thoughts were of murder, some were of a probable murderer who had now gone missing, some were of a certain painter and decorator who she definitely would meet for a drink that night. He'd texted her. She'd texted back. It had gone back and forth quite a bit, friendly, chatty, even playful. She was meeting him at eight in the Crown, if they could fight their way past the car enthusiasts.

But now, forcing herself into practical mode, she decided that she would use her time today to make up the dress she wanted to create for herself out of the fabric samples Oscar had given them. She'd found a pattern and Izzy had assured her that it would work well with the wool crepe.

She found that the dress was a simple design with relatively few pieces, and so the toile was complete by the time Izzy arrived at the shop.

"You've even put a zip in it!" said Izzy.

"I wanted to try it on and I couldn't figure out any other way to do up the back. I figured I could take the zip out afterwards and use it in the real garment," said Penny.

Izzy walked around her with pins and made some small adjustments to the fit. "This is going to look amazing in that wool crepe. You're having half in the turquoise and half in the shocking pink, yeah?"

Penny nodded.

"Did you know that we have shocking pink because of Elsa Schiaparelli?" said Izzy.

"The same one who made the lobster dress?"

"Yes. She made it popular back in the day, it was like her signature. I looked her up, she said it was impudent."

"Impudent, really?"

"Yes. It's a great colour and you should own it. Now, you will need to match the threads carefully when you're sewing to make sure it looks really polished. You might even want to stop halfway round when you're top stitching, so do half in the turquoise and half in the pink. But otherwise go for it. I'll mark up the fitting changes on the pattern and then you can crack on."

"Do you think I might be able to wear it today?" asked Penny.

"Yes, choose some lining fabric and get your head down. You can do this."

# 33

It was the first full day of the car show. There would be activities and music up at the field by the castle, but throughout the centre of the town classic cars had been parked, the roads shut to traffic and by mid-morning there were plenty of people ambling about, enjoying the vehicles and, of course, taking advantage of local pubs and cafés.

Izzy decided to take one of her parasols outside and demonstrate it more obviously. The sun was going to be strong today, and she hoped people would recognise the benefits of parasol ownership.

She strutted and twirled the parasol and wondered whether she needed a song and dance routine to draw the eye, but people were already looking.

One of the nearby cars had a Chitty Chitty Bang Bang look about it. She would have liked to know its model, but she concentrated hard on emitting a Truly Scrumptious vibe with her twirling.

"I say, that's a charming accessory!" called a man who was digging inside a picnic basket at the side of his chair. It looked as if the huge vintage car might be his.

Izzy went over. "I have a whole collection of these in the shop here. Each one is unique, but I call the collection Gardenia."

"Capital! How much is that one?"

Izzy didn't necessarily believe in exploiting the rich, but she made a spur of the moment decision that she could apply a delivery charge for people who lounged in the sunshine and said "Capital!" without irony. "Eighty five pounds."

The man reached for his wallet and fished out some notes. "Perfect. It will make for some very pretty pictures with the old gel."

Izzy wasn't at all sure whether he was talking about the car or an absent partner, but she smiled and nodded as she handed him the parasol.

She went back into the shop to put the money in the till.

"Did you sell a parasol?" asked Penny.

"I did!" said Izzy. "Maybe I need to match up a parasol with each of the cars outside and see if I can strike up conversations with the owners?"

They went to the window together to check out the cars on Market Hill.

"So, your frilly white ones will be the best bet for the most classic cars," said Penny, "but we've got some other types of cars, too. What would you call that one over there that looks as if it was made from the insides of a rusty dishwasher?"

The car was constructed along bold industrial lines and finished in a smudgy patchwork of orangey-browns.

"It's got a dystopian wasteland feel to it, like it belongs in Mad Max. What are the owners dressed like?"

Izzy couldn't see anyone there at the moment, but had she seen them at some point? "I did see a younger woman in a camouflage top and leather bikini bottoms. Maybe she's got something to do with it?"

They both turned to stare at the parasols.

"Did you make anything suitable?" asked Penny.

"Doesn't the very idea of a parasol sit awkwardly with a wasteland aesthetic?" Izzy said.

"Maybe we'll come back to that one. How about the camper vans? There are a couple of them and they both have a sort of sixties paint job."

"We've got the right shape," said Izzy. "A couple of these parasols are made from very deep cup-shaped umbrellas." She picked one up. "This one in sunflower yellow seems like it could work."

Izzy had a thought and she dipped into the box of oddments. "Somewhere in here are a couple of white daisies that would set it off nicely."

Penny helped her dig them out. There were three in total, about an inch and a half across. Izzy sewed them onto the parasol and gave it a twirl. "I'm going in!"

Izzy sauntered across the square with the parasol over her head.

"Oh hey!" she shouted to the two women who sat near

the camper vans. "I thought you might like to see this. It's like carrying your own personal store of sunshine. Have a go!"

The women looked at each other and smiled. One of them stood up. "I'll take a look."

Moments later she had another sale.

While she was out, Izzy continued to explore the car show. She walked with another of the parasols for her own pleasure. It was the blue chambray one with the fringe around the edges and it was fun to swish the ends back and forth as she ambled through the town.

The huge field near to the castle had many rows of cars, and it was at this point Izzy realised that she had barely seen a tenth of the car show. Many of the older cars were round here, and she saw a sign for a jumble sale, which sounded interesting. On closer inspection it was a jumble sale for bits and pieces of old cars and tools, but it seemed popular with the attendees.

There was a temporary stage and an organiser's tent set up in the most prominent area. Izzy saw Stuart Dinktrout, local business leader and owner of a most charming pot-bellied pig.

As he turned he noticed Izzy. She went over to say hello.

"Nice to see you here," she said.

"Well of course, it's important that I make myself available for events like this," he replied. "As chair of the chamber of commerce. I will of course be a part of the judging team later, but I am here to provide leadership as and when it's required."

"Ah I see," said Izzy. "Shame, I thought you might have brought Arabella along so that she could see the cars."

He nodded. "As you know, Arabella is a most intelligent pig and she has a keenly developed appreciation for the finer things in life. However I decided, on balance, that she would be better off left at home, as crowds do present a risk for a micro pig, as you can imagine. I could never live with myself if someone stepped on her."

Izzy smiled without voicing her thoughts on the matter. If she had been in charge of Arabella she would have come up with a solution, she thought. She would have brought the little pig round in her own trolley, or even in the front basket of her bicycle. Arabella would have enjoyed the chance to see the cars.

"Well, I hope that the judging goes well."

She had seen a leaflet somewhere that explained the categories of the car competition, but Izzy decided that it would be more interesting to go round and discover things for herself. It was clear that some of the cars were models that her parents might have seen on the roads, while others were much older. Some were faithfully restored and others looked as if they had been assembled by an overexcited magpie.

Wandering on from Stuart, Izzy was drawn to the more offbeat and creative vehicles. She drifted over to a car that reminded her of the carousel at fairs she had visited as a child. There was always a scramble to get the best vehicles. Squeezing into a shared space on the bus or in a jeep was everyone's last choice; the prime spots on the carousel were definitely the tiny plane, the daring motorbike or the jaunty roadster.

This car was painted a lurid purple colour with metallic

sparkles. Its wheels were cartoonishly huge in its wheel arches and the seats were upholstered in vibrant green plush fabric. Izzy automatically wanted to touch the upholstery but wasn't sure whether that would be frowned upon. The owner of the car was lolling in a deckchair nearby and wasn't even looking, so she reached through the open window and ran her fingers over the top of the seat. As she moved around the car she saw that it was a Hillman Imp fitted with a motorbike engine. She wondered what had inspired that choice, but the owner looked as if he was snoozing so she moved on.

Back in the town, one corner of the marketplace had the look and feel of a separate little encampment. There were five Land Rovers arrayed in an arc, each slightly different in the way it was painted and accessorised. One of the longer ones had luggage racks piled high with vintage cases, another was military green and very spartan, with only an old green fuel can as a visible accessory. Two were shorter with open tops and another was either completely unrestored or very artfully restored to look incredibly scruffy, Izzy couldn't tell. Their owners all clustered in the middle, sharing snacks from a coolbox. They wore matching t-shirts and Izzy wondered if it was an extended family group. She went over and saw that Tariq from the Frambeat Gazette was with them.

"Hey Izzy, come and meet the Sufflanders!" he said.

Izzy opened her mouth to ask what a 'Sufflander' was, then closed it upon noticing that the t-shirts were all emblazoned with Sufflanders! Suffolk's friendliest Land Rover club.

"Hi there!" she said to the group. "You all like Land Rovers, then?"

The man with the coolbox offered Izzy a can of Coke and nodded slowly. "It's not so much a question of liking them as being compelled to spend all of our time and money on them."

Izzy wondered if she was supposed to smile or laugh at that statement, but it seemed to have been offered as a serious explanation. "Well, they are very practical vehicles, I suppose."

"They *are* practical. Nothing stands in the way of a Land Rover!" said a woman leaning forward. "They all have their own characters and they tell us if they're not happy."

"How do they tell you?" Izzy asked.

The woman shrugged. "Black smoke, mechanical failure, that sort of thing."

At this the whole group laughed heartily.

"Oh, I think I see," said Izzy, "is that why you're a club, so that you can all come and rescue each other?"

"Oh yes," said the woman, "it's a very social thing."

"Monica's right," added the man. "We spend most of our free time together."

Izzy noticed Tariq's eyes shining as he snapped pictures and took notes. "Tariq, you look as though you're getting loads of good material from this corner of the show."

"It's all great background, Izzy. I've got some nice pictures of the vehicles and now I need to understand what lies beneath the surface."

"Very good." Izzy pulled Tariq aside with apologetic looks for the Sufflanders. "So, Tariq?"

"Yes?"

"This car show is journalistic gold, yeah?"

"I suppose so. Relatively speaking."

Izzy nodded in hearty agreement. "So maybe's it time to lay off with the investigations into the masked vandal stuff, yes?"

He pulled back, surprised. "But that's a genuine story." He waved his Access All Areas press pass at her. "Investigative journalism is a vital part of a functioning society."

"Yes. Yes. All true. But I fear that, since the masks came from our little shop — allegedly — that people might start harbouring negative thoughts towards us."

His frown deepened. "Are you asking me to sacrifice my journalistic values so you can make more money?"

"That is not what I'm saying," she said, firmly. "I'm saying take your pictures. Send them to me, even. I'd love to see them. Cars and fun and smiling faces. Find something else to grab your attention. A bit less of the mask story."

Tariq gave her a deeply doubtful look but she maintained her firm glare and moved on. She had seen someone she wanted to talk to.

# 34

Fliss Starling was walking across the square as if it were her own personal catwalk. She paused while someone took her picture, smiling and posing. Izzy hoped that Tariq had got a photo of Fliss in the lobster overall. It would be a useful boost for Cozy Craft's business and it would probably break up the endless pictures of cars in the souvenir edition.

Fliss waved to her, with the energy of a woman who might possibly have started drinking the summer cocktails early. She beamed widely. "This outfit is the best thing ever. I'm loving it!"

"You do look great," said Izzy.

Fliss had teamed the overall with a wide-brimmed hat so she wasn't in need of a parasol, but she pointed at the one that Izzy held. "Is this your work as well?"

Izzy nodded.

"Well, I hope you sell lots."

Fliss waved at someone over by the pub. "I must go and join my friends. Do you have time for a drink with us?"

Izzy looked round Fliss and saw that Carmella, Frank and Jacqui were sitting at a table outside the Crown. She waved at them too, and Carmella gave her a deep scowl.

"I'll just pop over and say hi. I'm not sure Carmella is a huge fan," said Izzy.

Fliss smiled. "She can be a little sour, it's true, but she is a pussycat once you get to know her. The japes we've shared, honestly!"

Izzy was intrigued. "Japes like what?"

"Oh, let me think. There was that time when we were all out together and us four girls went and swapped our tops over in the toilets to see if the fellas would notice. We did it four times, can you believe it? Four times, so we ended up back with our own tops and not one of them realised."

Izzy wasn't sure what response was appropriate. "Gosh," she said.

Fliss turned and wagged a finger. "You can guarantee that if we'd swapped something on their precious cars they would have spotted it instantly. It's all very telling!"

Izzy smiled at the group who had taken one of the wooden picnic benches next to the pub. "Hello everyone! I see Will's not here."

"A deep mystery," said Fliss.

"What? You've still not seen him? Since last night?"

Fliss pursed her lips.

"Man's got a lot on his mind," said Frank.

I bet he has, Izzy thought. She didn't know what she would have said to him if he had been there, anyway.

*"Hey, Will, is it true that you got up early and brained Derek with a spanner because he'd fathered a child with your wife and then you went back to bed before your wife realised you'd gone?"*

No, she couldn't quite imagine herself making such accusations. Surely the police would find this out themselves soon enough. Wouldn't they find Will's fingerprints on the deadly spanner? Unless he'd been wearing gloves. Or, indeed, they'd find his fingerprints but think nothing of it because it was his spanner.

She looked over to Will Starling's car, parked right outside the Crown Hotel. The long green piece of nineteen thirties luxury gleamed in the morning sun. Unlike many of the other owners, Will wasn't hanging around nearby to soak up the reflected admiration people might have for his vehicle.

"I hope he's all right," she said, neutrally.

"He's a big boy. He can cope," said Frank.

Izzy's hands caressed the car as she walked around it. She hovered over a patch of bodywork that seemed ever so slightly different to the rest, as though a mark had been touched up with fresh paint.

"Bird pooped on it?" called Frank.

"No. Just admiring the paintwork," said Izzy.

The difference between the new and the old paint was very, very subtle, but Izzy had an eye for colour.

In the window of the Derby Bentley was the official car show demonstrator's certificate and, next to that, a printed laminate with information about the make and model. Many of the cars on show had such information cards, providing a brief history as though these were indeed museum pieces.

Next to that card was a simple piece of A4 with a printed message that this car would be sold at auction, and the address for the auction company's website.

"Interesting," said Izzy. She smiled at the gathered friends and departed with a 'see you later' sort of wave

# 35

Penny constructed the main seams of her new dress in very little time. She was careful when it came to putting in the zip, knowing that it would make or break the look of the garment. Similarly, she made herself take the topstitching steadily, so that it was immaculate. She topstitched all around the contrasting panels of fabric, which gave the dress a very sleek look.

She went to try it on before turning up the hem. She slipped into it and felt a frisson of glee as the smooth lining slipped down and the dress sat neatly in place, skimming her hips. She trotted down to look in the mirror and grinned at her reflection.

Izzy appeared, looking over Penny's shoulder into the mirror.

"That is knockout! Let me get the pins and I'll put the hem up for you."

Penny loved the way that the two colours contrasted. It

pulled the eye but it didn't look weird or messy as she had feared it might. The boldness of the colours definitely suited her colouring, too.

"Now I'm not just trying to big you up here, but I reckon that looks better than the Dolce & Gabbana dress in Carmella's shop," said Izzy.

Penny wanted to twirl, but Izzy was busy with the hem and she risked getting jabbed with a pin. She could twirl later when she wore this glorious dress to meet Aubrey for drinks. It wasn't as if it was a date, but it was a great feeling to know that she was going to have a head-turning outfit to wear.

"Will Starling is selling his car," Izzy said as she worked.

"Yes?"

"He's got a sign on it and everything."

"Think that's linked to the murder?"

Izzy shook her head. "Can't see how. One's got nothing to do with the other, has it? But it's odd because, like the others, he clearly loves his car."

"Maybe he's going to buy an even posher one."

"Or he's clearing out the garage to make room for when he restores Monty's old car."

Monty the dog yipped.

"Would you like a big posh car of your own, would you? Would you?" said Izzy in a playful baby voice.

"How's parasol sales going?" Penny asked.

Izzy stood and then showed her the cash she'd already made that day.

"You're kidding! This is incredible, Izzy."

"I am incredible Izzy," she agreed. "Even better than

that," she added, glancing out through the window. "People are now checking out the parasols. I think we might see some customers coming to us." She pointed out to Penny the women by the camper van, who were demonstrating their lovely new yellow parasol to another woman wearing a tweed cap, and pointing over at the shop. "I suspect we're about to meet another customer for the Truly Scrumptious range."

Penny laughed and nodded. "I think you might be right."

They both watched as the woman came over and looked in the window. They withdrew discreetly but stole glances over at her as they went back to the counter.

"Oh hello," whispered Izzy. "Look who's also here."

Carmella had joined the woman outside the window, and they greeted each other as old friends. A few moments of pleasantries passed, and then Carmella's hand waved dismissively towards the window display.

"She's trying to talk her out of it!" hissed Penny. "How rude! She must know we can see her."

Carmella went a stage further and pulled out her phone, showing the screen to her friend.

"Oh yeah, now she's showing off her fake Bohemian parasols," said Izzy.

The exchange was still polite, but Izzy could see that the woman was becoming impatient with Carmella. She made a move towards the door of the shop. Carmella put a hand on her arm. It was a low-level attempt to restrain her, but the woman's face was furious. She slapped Carmella's hand away and strode into the shop.

Izzy wanted to applaud her, but luckily for them all,

Penny stepped over and greeted the woman warmly. "Hello, and how can we help you today?"

"I'm interested in your beautiful parasols," said the woman. "In fact," she glanced outside at Carmella, who was pretending not to watch, "I'm thinking of buying two of them."

# 36

After closing the shop on an interesting and reasonably lucrative day, Penny went upstairs to get changed. She wanted to jazz up her makeup and put on some shoes that would complement the dress. She had been fretting slightly about that, wondering if any of her footwear would work with it.

As she reached the top floor she saw something on the floor in front of the door to her room. It was a small box. She picked it up and opened it. There was a note on top.

*Your strappy t-bar sandals will work well with your new dress. Add these if you're feeling groovy! Love Izzy.*

Inside the box was a pair of embellishments. They were somewhere between a flower and a pom pom, and they were made from the scraps left over from her dress. Penny turned them over in her hands and saw that they featured a little strap and a press stud so that they could fit onto the middle of her sandals. She rushed into her room to try them out on her sandals and laughed out loud at how much fun they were.

When she was dressed she went outside, into the town. She was early for meeting Aubrey but she wanted to soak up some of the evening atmosphere from the car show.

Penny heard the sound of Carmella Mountjoy before she saw her. "Well! If this isn't the absolute limit!"

She turned with a smile. "Hello, Carmella."

In the evening light that cast a dramatic silhouette over St Michael's Church, Penny could see that Carmella was a more than a little worse for drink. A woman as skinny as that probably didn't have much capacity for alcohol, although Penny imagined she'd had plenty of practice. Frank Mountjoy was some distance back along the road, talking loudly with some chap by a fifties sports car.

"What do you call this?" asked Carmella, pointing up and down at Penny's dress.

Penny's brow crinkled. "I'm surprised you're not more familiar with dresses, Carmella, given you claim to run a shop that sells them." Her tone was harsher than it perhaps should have been, but Carmella Mountjoy was proving to be an insufferable pain.

"So this is your latest attempt to rip me off?"

"According to the sewing pattern, this is a classic design that every woman needs in their wardrobe," said Penny. "I think it looks very much like a Penny Slipper original, don't you? It's not even the same colour as the one in your shop."

"I saw you looking at it!" spat Carmella.

"How about this? If anyone sees my dress this evening

and asks where they can buy one, I will be sure to let them know about the one in your shop."

Carmella's mouth opened and closed again. She looked as if she wanted to complain, but seemed unable to muster a response that would suffice. She satisfied herself with a haughty twirl that took her off in the opposite direction. The haughty twirl would have worked much better if she'd not been so tipsy that she was forced to propel herself off a wall a moment later to avoid falling over.

"Everything alright?" said a voice directly behind Penny, making her jump.

## 37

"Sorry," said Aubrey. "Didn't mean to startle you."

Penny gave the big guy an embarrassed smile. "You following me?"

He tilted his head. "I was just heading into the Crown when I noticed you here in your..." He waved a hand at her attire. "... eye-catching dress. I thought you might have got lost."

"I was just taking a wander round town before coming to meet you."

"Ah. Still want to wander?"

"Maybe later," she smiled. "Drink?"

"Indeed."

The Crown was as busy this evening as it had been during the day. Penny bought drinks, a pint for Aubrey and a rum and coke for herself. and they found a space to sit in the rear courtyard of the hotel. Penny assumed that back in the days when this had been a coaching inn, stage coaches would have been able to drive right up to the rear of the building, possibly even through the frontage. Now, the courtyard was full of round tables, large potted plants and, currently, dozens of people chatting loudly and amiably following the first day of the car show.

"It's nice to see the town busy," he said, as they moved awkwardly through the throng to find seats.

"Being ironic?" said Penny as she popped out of the thickest press of bodies and put herself down at a table beneath a tall potted palm tree.

The evening was warm and the sky still held some light, with dangling strings of white lights hung in various positions around the courtyard to chase away the shadows.

Aubrey sipped the foamy head from his beer and shook his head.

"Towns like Fram need an influx of people to survive," he said. "We don't want to turn into yet another satellite housing estate for Ipswich or London. Too many places round here have been bought up as second homes by out-of-towners.

She arched an eyebrow at him.

"You're not an out-of-towner," he told her.

"I don't have the proper Suffolk accent," she said.

"Few do these days. You're a permanent fixture in this town now, right? Right?"

She didn't want to tell him that she still had a place in London, and friends there too. She didn't want to tell him that once Nanna Lem had properly recovered the use of her leg, the natural thing for her to do would be to go back to the great metropolis.

"I feel I fit in here," she said. "There's enough going on to keep me interested."

"Making Dali-inspired dresses and such?"

"The customer was very impressed," she said. "The drinks tonight are very much on Cozy Craft, as a thank you to you."

"I've not done painting of an artistic sort for years."

"Your lobster was very good."

"I should branch out into all manner of crustaceans," he said. "Course, I was reading up on it and Salvador Dali's work was all about symbolism. Nothing in his pictures was what it looks like it's meant to be. Those dribbling melting clocks of his. I read that he was inspired to paint them while looking at soft French cheese, and that they're supposed to represent Einstein's theories about time or something. And most of his pictures of animals and food and things had a somewhat" — his voice dropped to a whisper — "sexual meaning."

"You are allowed to say that word out loud," Penny smiled. "I suspect our customer was thoroughly familiar with the symbolism associated with her outfit. In fact, I suspect she might be something of a car widow."

There were perhaps a couple of heads turned towards her from other tables at that point. Car widows or indeed the car-loving widow-makers, wondering what she was saying.

"She might be an older woman, but I think she would rather have had some attention lavished on her that he was otherwise giving to his car."

"See?" said Aubrey. "I was thinking you were just making

a dress for the woman but it turns out there was some whole other symbolic meaning to the enterprise."

"I imagine the secret symbolism went straight over the man's head. He was happy enough to fund his wife's requests, but he didn't seem to be paying much attention to what was right in front of him." A thought crossed her mind.

"What is it?" said Aubrey, reading her expression.

"When the customer picked up the dress, she had to search through her credit cards to find the ones that would be able to cover the bill."

"There was a danger she wasn't going to pay?"

"And the husband, Will Starling, has put his classic car up for sale. It's the big green Bentley just in the marketplace outside."

"Musing on other people's financial problems, are we?"

She wanted to tell him that wasn't exactly it. Except it sort of was. She leaned in close, and when he didn't mirror her, put her hand on his shoulder and pulled him into proper whispering range.

"You know the murder up at Saxtead Grange?" she said.

"Burglary gone wrong, wasn't it?" said Aubrey.

She shook her head. "We think —"

"This is Izzy and you?"

"Yes. We think Will Starling did it. Maybe because the victim had an affair with Will's wife."

"The victim had an affair with lobster lady?"

"Years ago. Yes. Maybe. And the interesting thing is, no one has seen Will since yesterday morning when he brought his car up here."

Aubrey gave this due thought.

"And you're trying to solve his murder because..."

"Because it's one of things going on in the town that particularly interests me." She leaned back. "And because some of the youngsters we gave masks to at the party on Tuesday have been right little terrors since."

"Oh, I've seen the posters that eager journalism student has put up," he said. "Silly rumours. They travel fast in a small town. One of your masked tikes getting the blame for the murder?" He drained the last of his pint. "Another?"

"Er, I'm paying for the drinks tonight, remember?" she reminded him.

"You can pay for them if you wish," he said cheerily. "I'm just offering to push through the rugby scrum to get them."

The crowds were indeed thick. Penny shrugged and gave Aubrey her bank card. "Don't go spending it all at once."

He turned sideways and slid through the mass of bodies, as if he was pushing his way through thick forest.

Thoughts of money turned Penny's mind back to the Bentley. She took out her phone and searched for Derby Bentleys up for auction. She soon found Will Starling's car on a British auction site. The on-line auction was still in progress, but she found links to the few other Derby Bentleys that had been sold in recent years. She searched on, checking those prices against each other, unable to quite believe what she was reading.

Aubrey burst from the crowd.

"You'll never guess how much Will Starling's car is worth," she said, before she realised that Aubrey didn't have any drinks in his hand.

"Quick!" he said. "You have to come with me!"

He held out his hand and without thinking or wondering why, she took it. He pulled her out and over to the rear gates of the courtyard.

"Quicker to go round than back through!" he said.

He was bouncing as he moved, as if he were having to stop himself from breaking into a run.

"I don't run well in sandals," she said. "What is it? Did you pick a fight with someone? Are we running away?"

He passed a brown leather wallet to her.

"What is it?" she said.

"As I was going to the bar, a bunch of people got up from one of the tables nearby. The barmaid was pulling my pint when I noticed this on the floor under the table. I showed it to the barmaid and she opened it and..."

Penny opened the wallet. The topmost bank card belonged to a Mr William Starling.

"This is Will's wallet."

"The murderer? Right?" said Aubrey.

"I asked the barmaid. She said she didn't know any of the men, but they were going up to the castle field. I said I'd take his wallet back to him."

"Are we chasing a murderer?" said Penny.

"I don't know. Are we?"

Fore Street at the back of the Crown had a side turning down into Crown and Anchor Lane which became a narrow passageway between buildings. They hurried down, onto Church Street, and cut up right towards the castle.

"What does he look like?" asked Aubrey.

"Tall. Grey-haired. Looks like he owns a posh old car."

"That describes quite a few people around this weekend," said Aubrey.

"I've seen him in a blue drivers cap, like one of those ones old-fashioned delivery boys used to wear."

"Uh-huh."

The pavements up to the castle were reasonably full with people, and from the field in front of the gargantuan castle there came the sound of music. The area was floodlit, the cars parked all around the edge of the field illuminated in the deepening night. The marquee in the centre of the field was busy. Catchy swing music, the woodwind and brass batting the tune back and forth amongst themselves, filled the air.

"We'll check here and then we'll check the beer tent," said Aubrey, having to raise his voice a little to be heard.

Penny didn't want to ask what they would do if they found Will, other than presenting him with his wallet.

They pressed into the marquee. Penny cast about for sight of Will. Aubrey repeatedly pointed men out to her with a "Is that him? Is that him?" and Penny had to shake her head every time. The centre of the tent was given over to a dance floor. There were plenty of swing dancers (or maybe they were lindy hoppers, Penny wasn't sure) and nearly all were dressed in period-appropriate clothing. A-line skirts and beautiful blouses abounded, as did waistcoats and ties. In the whirl of people having fun, Penny saw a familiar purple felt hat whisk by, but when she tried to follow it, it had gone.

Aubrey tugged at her arm.

"Let's try the beer tent," he said. She had to lip-read over the music but understood him well-enough.

They pushed their way out and over to the tent where a local brewery was doling out plastic cups of beer to those enjoying the night-time fun. They walked round and through and made several circuits.

"You know," said Penny eventually, "we don't have to spend our Saturday evening trying to chase down a murderer."

"The fact that you can utter such an incredible sentence is one of the things that makes you fun," said Aubrey.

But it seemed clear that Will Starling, wherever he had gone after leaving the Crown, had not come here.

"Fine," Aubrey sighed. "We'd best take the wallet back to the Crown and let them hold onto it."

He reached out a hand to her. She took it. There was no urgency in the handholding now, but there was a quiet electricity that made Penny smile.

# 38

Izzy took Monty out for an early Sunday morning walk before the start of the second full day of car-related events. It was going to be busy in the town with all of the motor show comings and goings, so it made sense to stretch his little legs while it was quieter. There were plenty of other dog walkers doing the same thing, so the dogs would stop and exchange greetings by way of their sniffing and tail-wagging rituals.

They met another corgi, and Izzy watched closely. Did Monty relate to other corgis more than he would other breeds? It seemed as though the ritual was much the same. She glanced up at the woman with the other dog and exchanged a few words of greeting.

"Morning."

"Morning."

"What's yours called?" asked the woman with the corgi.

"Monty."

"This is Death Row."

"Um, is it?"

"So nice for two corgis to meet, isn't it?" said the woman.

"In the circumstances, yeah. I'm so very sorry. Is there nothing that we can do?" Izzy asked.

"Do about what?" asked the woman.

"Death row. You mean that he's going to be put down, yeah?" Izzy said, feeling her throat constrict mournfully at the prospect.

The woman stared open-mouthed at Izzy. "His name is Jethro. With a J. Did you think I said —" She was unable to suppress a laugh, and doubled over with merriment. "Death row!"

Izzy was horrified at her mistake, but delighted that the dog would live. A maelstrom of conflicting emotions swept through her, but the mirth on the woman's face was infectious. She joined her in laughing at her mistake and then patted Jethro on the head.

"So happy that you're going to be alright, little fella!"

She walked on, laughing every time she remembered her mistake. She thought that she could hear Jethro's owner doing the same as she walked off in the opposite direction.

"Death row!" she heard in the distance. "Wait 'til I tell your dad."

Izzy returned to the shop with Monty.

"Hey Monty! Did you have fun on your walk?" said Penny in the special voice she reserved especially for Monty. Izzy suspected that her cousin, who perhaps would normally have regarded this creature as both a distraction and an unnecessary expense, was becoming attached to the bundle of fur. "What you got there, boy?"

Izzy tutted. "He found this brush by the bins and he won't let go of it." It was a long-handled plastic brush, the sort that might be used for washing-up. Its bristles were small stumpy remnants and now, apparently, it was a chew toy. "He seems to like it."

"It's a bit yucky though," said Penny. "Maybe I should get him a proper toy from the pet shop?"

"Why would we spend our money on a dog toy when we could make one, Penny?"

"We used up all the scraps on his bed, though," said Penny.

"Ah Penny, just because the scrap bin is empty doesn't mean we're out of scraps." Izzy smiled. "We have a few rolls of vintage fabric that's a bit too faded or stained to sell as first quality."

The shop was mostly ship-shape, but there were still several rolls of material taking up space where they weren't strictly supposed to. Izzy popped upstairs and came back down with the big roll of creamy Laura Ashley print.

"I used some of it for my skirt. Jacqui Bildeston said some very complimentary things about it," said Izzy. "Can't use the full width as it's been stored in sunlight and it's half faded."

"Must have been expensive to buy a bolt of that stuff and then not use it," said Penny.

"Nanna Lem had her reasons."

"Not all of them sane."

"It's interesting in its own way," said Penny.

"So what sort of toy should we make for our Monty?"

Penny thought for a moment. "Since he's probably just going to savage it, maybe we should keep it simple."

"We should make what we want."

"I think he would like a rabbit. A fat body and long ears." She sketched out an imaginary image with her fingertips.

Izzy passed her some tailor's chalk. "Draw it for real. Keep it simple and bold."

Penny did as Izzy suggested. She made some corrections, dusting the chalk with a hand to erase her mistakes. "Like that?"

Izzy nodded. She cut out around the shape, adding a seam allowance as she went. She then flipped it over and cut a mirror image copy.

"Here we go, Monty, this is going to be for you!" she said as she took it over to the sewing machine and sewed around the edges.

Izzy spent a few minutes cutting the rest of the cotton fabric into shapes, trimming off some of the frayed edges.

"So, how was last night's date?" she asked casually.

"Wasn't a date."

"Sorry. Drinks with a man whose hunky body does something squiggly to your insides."

"Not that, either. Not quite. It was nice. Hey — funny thing happened. Will Starling left his wallet in the Crown. We chased after him but must have lost him on the castle field."

"Uh-huh. So you went chasing after our number one murder suspect?"

"Sort of murder suspect. The one that best fits our theory. Do you know how much his Bentley might go for?"

"A quarter of a million," said Izzy as she stuffed the off-cuts inside the rabbit body.

"You know?"

"I looked it up."

"Me too," said Penny. "Two hundred and fifty thousand pounds. Or more. That's a lot of money for a car."

"Particularly if your wife is struggling to find a credit card that's not maxed out."

"Exactly."

"Do you know what I find most worrying about all of that?" said Izzy.

"What?"

"On your date not-a-date with Aubrey, the most interesting thing you have to report is that you chased down a man you couldn't find."

"The evening was perfectly lovely."

"You two hit it off?"

"You know we get along."

"Yeah, but did you...?" Izzy left the question hanging but annoyingly, Penny refused to play along.

"We're not school kids, Izzy. Aubrey and I had a very nice evening, thank you. Have you finished sewing that?"

Izzy had indeed nearly finished the sewing on the rabbit.

"Do you want to do the honours?" she asked Penny, handing the toy over.

"Oh yes, thank you." Penny waggled the rabbit in front of Monty. "Here we are, a new toy for you! How about I give you this and you let go of that weird brush?"

Monty looked up and wagged his tail lazily as he reclined

on his dog bed, but he made no move to let go of the brush, which remained firmly clamped between his teeth.

"Look, this is so cute! It's a wascally wabbit!" Penny tried out a cartoon voice to tempt Monty, but he kept up the polite, dutiful wag, while hanging onto his brush.

"Maybe leave it there. He'll take a look when he's ready," said Izzy.

Penny sighed and left the rabbit next to Monty while he chomped happily on the handle of the old brush.

"I hope we get plenty of passing trade today again," she said.

"Maybe sell the last of these parasols," said Izzy.

"You walking up and down and twirling them seemed to be quite effective," Penny pointed out.

"I'm happy to go do some twirling," Izzy conceded.

# 39

With a funky sunflower parasol over her shoulder, Izzy made a loop around the car show. Some of the narrow streets had a line of cars right down the centre. Getting everyone into place must have required strong organisational skills, with everyone arriving at the right time and taking their place without blocking access for others. If any of these cars wanted to move before the end of the show they would be out of luck.

She realised that along Castle Street there was a line of very small cars. She looked more closely and saw that each one in this line of about twelve was based on the same toy. They had existed for years and were made by one of the big manufacturers out of robust plastic. By the row of cars was a sign that proudly proclaimed the display as Cosy Coupe Alley. Cosy Coupes were the almost unbreakable kiddies cars that she remembered, but these were very different. All had been resprayed, and many of them somehow had alloy wheels. There were vans, tractors and police cars. Each one appeared to be still useable as a toy. In fact, their owners looked to be mostly parents, accompanied by children grinning proudly at the passers-by.

Izzy stopped at one that had lowered suspension and blue downlights shining from underneath. "This still works as a car, yeah?" she asked the man who sat alongside.

His daughter, a girl of about six, answered. "Of course it works! You should see it in the dark."

"Huh. It's pretty amazing," said Izzy. "How on earth do people get these alloy wheels?"

"Everyone uses steel bowls," said the girl. "You can get them in the pet shop. The ones for cats are the right size. My dad cuts the wheels so that the pet bowl sits inside and he drills a hole for the axle, see?"

Izzy did see, As she looked along the line she could see that the pet bowl idea was in use on most of the cars. "Well I never. You have a very cool ride there, thanks for bringing it along."

"You're welcome," said the girl, patting the roof of her car with pride.

Izzy doubled back, cut through the churchyard and back into the marketplace.

There was a surprising sight over in the enclave of Land Rover owners. Tariq from the paper was there, sitting in a chair of his own, and now wearing one of the club's t-shirts.

"Tariq?" Izzy said.

He looked up from the computer tablet they were all poring over. "Oh hi, Izzy! Monica thinks I should get a long wheel base model, but the twins are all about the short wheel bases. What do you think?"

"Huh?"

"It's not that much to get a vintage Land Rover, I had no idea!"

"I had no idea you were interested."

"Just introducing the lad to the wonderful world of Land Rover ownership," said the large chap beside him.

"Tariq, maybe I could have a brief word," said Izzy.

"Hmmm?"

"Over here," she said, beckoning furiously.

He wandered over to her, looking backwards at his new friends.

"Can you even drive?" Izzy asked him.

"Well, no, but apparently you learn really quickly in a vehicle like this because —"

"You need to step away and take some deep breaths," she said.

"I'm just getting caught up in the fun and —"

"Precisely. I think you might have been swept along by the enthusiasm that your new friends have. I'm not usually the one to say this, but don't do anything rash!"

"You told me to find something else to interest me."

"I didn't tell you to buy a Land Rover. Besides, you're meant to be taking pictures of the show."

"I've taken thousands. I've mailed a link to the upload folder to you. I've been doing nothing but take pictures since early Friday when the cars started arriving."

"Right," she said. "I'm just suggesting that you take a

break from…" She jiggled her parasol at the Land Rover fans. "… from all that."

Tariq gave her a crestfallen nod. "It would be so nice to belong to their group."

"Ask them if you can belong while you're still thinking about a vehicle," said Izzy. "I'm sure you'll be welcome."

She watched him walk off. She understood the allure of fun vintage machines, she really did. She'd have to see if Tariq would like to tinker with an old sewing machine.

# 40

Penny's phone buzzed and she saw that she had a message from Nanna Lem.

*You are bringing something over for the tombola, aren't you?*

"Oh crumbs!" Penny had completely forgotten. Miller Fields sheltered accommodation would have its doors open during the motor show today. Whether it was an attempt to drum up new business or to join in the fun, Penny wasn't certain, but she had promised Nanna Lem a tombola prize.

"Prizes, prizes." She scanned the shop. Obviously, they had lots of dressmaking bits and bobs in here but they wouldn't make a decent prize. If she had some unwanted Christmas gifts, like bath salts or oils, they would have been ideal. But nothing came to mind. There was the jacket Izzy had stolen off a scarecrow, but clothes weren't exactly the kind of thing for a tombola stall.

Penny's gaze moved to the rabbit beside Monty's dog bed. It still looked untouched. Had Monty taken any interest in it at all? Not that she'd noticed, whereas the nasty brush was still clearly a big hit.

Penny picked up the rabbit, knowing that she had taken one step towards a course of action that she hadn't yet admitted to herself. She brushed off imaginary dog hairs, but really, this was just a perfectly sweet rabbit soft toy. She turned it over and made sure there were no marks. Once she had established that it would pass as a new toy, Penny went all-in. She fetched a paper bag from the till and popped the rabbit inside. Then she thought about it and fetched it out again. She added a tag, so that everyone would know it had come from Cozy Craft.

Penny closed the shop, leaving a '*back in 10 minutes*' sign on the door, and took the rabbit round to Miller Fields before she lost her nerve.

She cut across Market Hill, squeezing round the morning crowd and then over into Fore Street. The roads here were much quieter. No matter how busy the heart of Fram became, that sense of busyness never stretched far from the centre.

The doors of the Miller Fields sheltered accommodation building were open. There was a welcoming balloon arch and, through another set of doors, Penny could see that a small indoor fete had been set up. There was a cake stall, a guess the number of sweets in the jar stall and a pair of tables laden with cheap and eclectic prizes in front of a tumbling tombola drum.

The stall was currently being manned by Glenmore Wilson, centre resident and one of the volunteers on the Frambeat Gazette.

Penny jiggled her rabbit. "I was looking for my Nanna Lem."

"A prize for the tombola?" said the man. His somewhat severe expression didn't shift much.

"Er, yes."

"I think Lem is still in her apartment. Resting."

"Right." She backed away and went off to Nanna Lem's flat.

"It's open," Nanna Lem called when Penny knocked.

Nanna Lem was standing in the hallway. As she saw Penny, she winced in pain and reached for her walking stick.

"You all right?" said Penny.

"Comes and goes," replied Nanna Lem, giving her bad leg a weak wiggle. "Just putting some lippy on before going down to the open day."

"Looks like it's going to be a success," said Penny, and then held up the rabbit toy.

"For the stall? Oh, that does look nice," said Lem. "I ordered in some Laura Ashley with that very same pattern."

"Well, yes."

"Ah," said the older woman. "At least it's getting some use. Will you walk me down?"

"Of course."

As they moved to the door together, Penny glanced through to the lounge area and the purple felt hat on the arm of the sofa.

"I saw a hat just like that last night," she said.

"Like what? Like that?" Nanna Lem grunted. "Izzy got it for me. They probably make millions of them."

"Perhaps."

It was slow progress to the community room. Penny hadn't realised how slow Nanna Lem had become since her accident back in the winter. The older woman leaned heavily on her as she walked. Penny couldn't imagine her being fit and healthy enough to resume her duties at the shop.

"We were talking about Gertie Masters the other day," said Nanna Lem.

"We were," said Penny.

"I bought the Laura Ashley print in for her. It was the favourite of a friend of hers."

"Really?"

"Because you were wondering why I had bought a fabric that I'd not used or sold."

"Well, yes, I was."

"But she died before she could collect it."

Penny hummed to herself. "Monty and Gertie were on their way into Fram when the accident happened. Might she have even been on her way to collect it?"

"I don't know," Lem said candidly. "It's a long time ago now and I don't know if I even heard about her death until several days later. It's not like today when everything's on Facebook the moment it happens."

They shuffled into the community room and Nanna Lem dropped gratefully into a chair next to Glenmore Wilson.

"Have we worn your grandmother out?" he said.

Nanna Lem shushed him and then took the rabbit from Penny once more. "This does look lovely. Would you be a dear and fetch me a cup of tea? Glenmore?"

"I've had my daily allowance of caffeine already," he said.

As Penny gladly went off to get her grandma a cuppa, Lem and Glenmore fell into a sort of bickering chat. They looked like an old married couple, but then again, so many older people did seem to talk as if all the social filters they'd built up in life had been eroded in later years.

Nanna Lem had finished putting a ticket on the rabbit when Penny returned from the refreshments stand.

"So, Gertie Masters and Monty Bildeston?" Penny asked.

"Yes?" said Nanna Lem.

"They were possibly just driving into town on a secret birthday mission to pick up fabric with which Gertie could sew something for Jacqui? She's the one who loved that pattern."

"I suppose."

This presented certain things in a new light to Penny. Nanna Lem studied Penny's face.

"You thought they were having a bit of a fling, didn't you?"

"I didn't. I mean I did. But I thought I might be jumping to conclusions."

Nanna Lem tutted and nudged Glenmore. "Young people today. They think everything's about sex. Can't imagine people just being friends or a married couple being faithful and devoted to each other."

"I don't think that's true," said Penny, although her imagination had certainly drifted in that direction.

"I believe that Monty and his wife — Jacqui, was it? — I believe they loved each other dearly. Don't be so swift to dismiss old fashioned love and affection."

"Hear, hear," said Glenmore. "Now, are you going to buy a tombola ticket, miss?"

# 41

Penny walked back to the shop. Izzy was at the counter flicking through images on the shop tablet.

"Gertie and Monty weren't having an affair," Penny said, slightly breathless.

The corgi bounced round her feet, excited.

"Not you, Monty," Penny told him, and fussed him.

Izzy looked up briefly. "They weren't?"

"Possibly not. That bolt of Laura Ashley. Gertie was going to use it to make Jacqui a surprise present from Monty."

"Doesn't mean they *weren't* having an affair."

"But it does present a perfectly innocent explanation for a man and a woman with other spouses elsewhere to be unexpectedly in a car together."

"True, true," said Izzy. She gestured to the tablet. "Tariq has sent me the pictures he's taken of the motor show so far. When he said he'd taken thousands I thought he must be exaggerating, but he wasn't.

Thought I might catch a glimpse of Will in one of them, work out where he went after dropping off the car."

"Good idea."

"Think I'm getting a repetitive strain injury from too much swiping."

"I can take over if you like."

"Okay. And I'll put the kettle on for a cuppa."

"I think we're out of biscuits," said Penny.

"Who's eaten them all?" asked Izzy, scandalised.

"I think Aubrey found painting lobsters hungry work. Oh, and I think someone — naming no names — has been sneakily giving digestives to the dog."

Izzy said nothing and went to the upstairs kitchenette.

Penny called up after her. "Oh! I know what I meant to ask you. Where did you get that hat from, the purple one that Nanna Lem loves?"

"I made it," Izzy shouted back down. "She loves purple and she loves wool felt, so I combined the two into that hat for her birthday a year or two back."

"You sure?"

Izzy popped her head round from the bottom of the stairs. "Yes, I'm sure. You never forget something you've made."

"How very strange," said Penny. "I saw a similar one yesterday and Nanna Lem said you'd bought it for her, not made it."

"Forgetfulness in her old age?" Izzy suggested.

"Nanna Lem is as sharp as a tack."

Izzy shrugged. "I bet she let one of her friends borrow it

and didn't want to tell you. I must tell her to watch out for catching nits."

"Nits? Really?"

"Yep. She used to get on at me all the time. Insisted it was wrong to share hats because of nits."

Penny sighed. "Were you at primary school at the time, Izzy?"

Izzy screwed up her face, trying to remember. "Yeah, maybe. You think the rules are different for adults?"

"Yes. Yes, they are."

Izzy's frown didn't go away. It deepened further. "I need to check on something," she said. "I'm just going out for a bit."

"Are you checking on Nanna Lem's hat?"

"No. Something else. A niggle in my brain." She headed for the door. "And I'll buy biscuits while I'm out."

Penny swiped through the many, many pictures on the tablet. Izzy's friend Tariq had indeed taken thousands of photographs and in many of them, he'd caught the gleam and the style and the beautiful designs that made certain cars so attractive. The rear tail fins of a mid-century American open top car. The shiny brass headlight mountings of a much older British car. And he'd captured the people, too. People laughing and joking, people posing by their vehicles.

She laughed out loud when she saw he had several pictures of Fliss Starling in her beach pyjama overalls with the Dali-style lobster painted down the leg. Fliss had her head tossed back, enjoying the attention. It was a great picture. Penny made a mental note to ask for a copy. They could put it up somewhere in the shop.

Swiping further, travelling back into Friday morning, she saw pictures of the cars arriving, images of vehicles before they were surrounded by people and other cars. As she swiped past the curved bonnet of a grey post-war car she saw Will Starling's green Bentley in the background. She looked at the time stamp on the picture. It wasn't even nine o'clock on Friday morning. Will had been up early.

She swiped back further. Green Bentley, green Bentley, no green Bentley. The time stamp was eight thirty. She swiped forward again and scoured the pictures.

"There!"

The picture was focused on the car in foreground, but there was a figure behind it, by the Bentley, slightly blurred. It was almost certainly Will Starling. He had his little blue driving cap on his head and, in matching tweed...

Penny stopped. She looked over to the side shelf where they'd put the jacket Izzy had borrowed off a scarecrow. She looked at the picture and the jacket.

"Wait, wait, wait," she said, confused.

Monty, in his basket and still merrily chewing a horrid old brush, tilted his head at her in a questioning manner.

"On Wednesday morning, Jacqui goes out and punches a scarecrow which Frank mistakes for the killer. Friday morning, Will drives into town to park his car wearing his jacket. That same morning, Izzy walks Monty —"

The dog barked.

"Yes, you," said Penny. "You walked across the fields and Izzy borrowed this jacket — this very jacket! — from the same scarecrow. So the jacket wasn't on the scarecrow before

Friday morning because Will was wearing it. And that means..."

She didn't know what that meant. It surely meant something and she didn't think it meant anything good.

"Monty. Let's grab your lead and go look at a scarecrow."

## 42

Izzy walked, not with a purpose but with the energy of a woman whose head was full of something. She walked through the town, past the cosy coupes and the twentieth century sports cars and the custom-built oddities. From the direction of the castle field came the soft warbling of a PA system. They were building up to prize-giving part of the car show weekend.

Walking did not make the answers come, but Izzy allowed the ideas to percolate in her brain. She did all her best thinking while not actually trying to think. The clearest ideas and cleverest notions tended to pop into her head while she was doing something else entirely.

Penny had mentioned Nanna Lem's hat, the one that Nanna Lem simply knew Izzy had made for her. And yet Nanna Lem had lied about where it had come from. Swapping hats with other people? It was like that thing Fliss Starling had said the other day, about the 'japes' she,

Carmella, Jacqui and Gertie had performed, swapping clothes and their men being none the wiser.

Up ahead, at the corner of Double Street, a masked figure leapt out with a yell at a woman. It was the little Jean Luc Picard that Derek had mistaken for Telly Savalas.

"Theodore!" the woman snapped. "Stop trying to scare us! It doesn't work!"

"Who is this Theodore of whom you speak?" the little bald menace declared haughtily.

"I can tell it's you!" the mother snapped, grabbed his hand and hauled him along with her.

Izzy would have laughed if the whole masked menace issue wasn't such a sore point at that moment.

Although the husbands hadn't spotted their wives changing tops, a mother could spot her own child beneath any mask. But it was just like Fliss had said. "*You can guarantee that if we'd swapped something on their precious cars they would have spotted it instantly.*"

And that was the thought that stopped Izzy dead.

"Oh," she said and then, because that didn't seem enough, added another emphatic, "Oh!"

"Are you all right, love?" said a passing woman.

"I've no idea," said Izzy and all but ran back to Market Hill.

She went to Will Starling's car outside the Crown and ran her hands over it, searching, searching...

There it was! The patch of green paint that didn't quite match the rest, nearly but not perfectly. It was just a small patch, a hasty repair. Izzy looked around to see if people were watching but, of course, there were people everywhere. It couldn't stop her.

She dipped into her purse, took out her keys and, with only a moment's hesitation, scratched at the paintwork. The keys bit deep and on the second stroke, a whole flaky chunk fell away.

Underneath was a separate layer of red paint. Bright, vibrant, almost a lobster red.

Izzy gave a strangled squeal of excitement. This explained everything. She thought for a second. Yes. Everything.

# 43

It was a mildly arduous walk across the ploughed loam of the fields. In the wide Suffolk skies, flat-bottomed clouds painted a scene across the blue heavens but the sun shone through and Penny was soon warm.

"Much further, is it?" she asked Monty.

Monty strained at the lead as though in answer.

The scarecrow was on a rise at the next corner in the hedgerow. It rested at a jaunty angle on its pole. Gravity had made its plastic container head tilt the other way, giving the impression it was peering round a corner. There, on the scarecrow's head, on top of its thatch of straw hair, was a blue cap. Whether one called it a newsboy cap or a driving cap, it was indeed the very cap Penny had seen in the picture and had seen more than once on Will Starling's head.

She lifted it up and inspected the inside, as if expecting to find a name tag.

"So what does all this mean?" she said.

Monty ignored her and sniffed at a dandelion.

She pondered.

"Will came into town early on Friday and parked his car. And then, because the car is still there, he must have walked back across the fields, leaving his cap and jacket here before... well, disappearing completely." She checked herself. "No. He was at the pub last night." She checked herself again. "His *wallet* was at the pub last night."

Dandelion business finished, Monty pulled onward.

"You're not helping me solve this, Monty," she told him. "Why would he leave his car in town, and his wallet too, and then abandon his coat and jacket here? Did he want people to think he was in town when he wasn't?"

She recalled the picture of the out-of-focus figure by the Bentley.

"Or... *someone* wanted people to think Will was in town when he wasn't. They drove in super early, wearing his hat and jacket as a disguise, which would only work if people didn't see him close up, wouldn't it? But it would work, sort of, I guess. And someone would want people to think Will was in town because..."

Monty was pulling towards what Penny could now see was a gap in the hedge ahead. Beyond the gap were the gardens of Saxtead Grange.

"Someone wanted people to think Will was in town because he wasn't," Penny said. "He was here. All along."

She pushed through the hedge and into the offensively huge gardens of the old manor house. The long fishing pond was off to one side, the house to the other.

Assuming he was guilty of killing Derek, Penny couldn't

imagine why Will would try to hide out at his own home. It was the first place the police would look. And it would require all the other residents to be his accomplices. No, that didn't work.

She saw the sagging washing line and remembered Izzy's mention of the stolen clothes line prop. Odd details. Strange facts. There were too many elements to this weird puzzle. Scarecrows and masks and people playing silly beggars with dropped wallets. Simple explanations were always the best but nothing was simple here. Who stole huge poles when there was nowhere to hide them? Who faked a man's presence in a town when, at that time, no one was looking for him?

Knowing she was trespassing, she walked further round the house to where they had previously met Fliss Starling. The iron chairs and table stood unoccupied on the lawn, a little distance up from the well. Here, Fliss had outlined her desires for a new dress — money no object, Will had said — while Derek shouted for his dog and Carmella shouted at him to be quiet.

Friendship groups were odd things. After knowing each other for decades these people were capable of antagonising each other on a daily basis whilst still claiming to be the best of friends.

"Ah," she said as a thought entered her mind.

Perhaps it had been the sight of the scarecrow with its supporting pole running up its trouser leg that had prompted the thought, but she realised there was probably one place you could easily hide a long clothes prop out here. She walked across to the well, stood carefully at the edge of the low stone wall, and looked down. It was deep, dark and there was no sign of a bottom or even water at the base. She peered around the edges, wondering if she might spot the top of the line prop leaning up against the side.

Monty put his paws on the wall, his tongue lolling.

"Hang on," said Penny. She took out her phone and turned on the torch function to shine a light into the dark.

# 44

Izzy rushed back to tell Penny everything and was surprised to find the shop locked up with the 'back in 10 minutes' sign up.

"Well, where are you?" she declared to no one at all.

She unlocked the door and went inside. Penny was not there, nor Monty.

"An emergency walk?"

She took out her phone and called Penny.

Penny's phone buzzed as she tried to shine a light down the well, causing her to nearly fumble and drop it. She pulled back, saw it was Izzy and clicked onto speaker phone before angling her torch down again. Brickwork that had never seen the light of day was revealed in stark light.

"Hi Izzy. Sorry. Monty and I just had to pop out."

"Had to?"

"Yes. We're at Saxtead Grange and something just occurred to me —"

"What are you doing?" a voice demanded stridently from behind Penny.

Penny gave a start, and this time she *did* fumble her phone. Seeing everything that was going to happen just before it occurred, Penny watched her phone slip, reached out her hand to try to catch it and all but batted it away, down the deep well.

The light strobed as the spinning phone fell.

It clattered on the wall, bounced off the line prop wedged at an angle near the bottom, and then plopped into shallow water.

The electronics only lasted a moment or two before the water destroyed them, but that was enough time for Penny to see, in the cold torchlight, the twisted legs and body of the corpse at the bottom of the well.

IN THE COZY CRAFT SHOP, Izzy stared at her phone and the dropped call. She'd heard the voice. She'd heard a clatter. Terrible and wild possibilities stormed her mind.

"Oh, no. Oh, no. This is not good. Not good."

She looked about herself.

"Who are you talking to, Izzy?" she demanded and hurried out of the shop once more.

Saxtead Grange was a forty minute walk, a twenty minute cycle. It was too long. It would take her far too long. Thoughts of Penny in non-specific danger almost overwhelmed her.

She needed to get up there, and she needed to get up there quickly, but she didn't have a car and, even if she did, the roads were thronged with people.

And then, as if summoned by her panic, the answer appeared to her. She ran over to the Land Rover enclave in the corner. She looked at the Sufflanders.

"Monica, isn't it?" she said.

"That's right," said the woman, biting into a bacon butty someone had just passed her.

"Nothing stands in the way of a Land Rover, you said."

"Possibly," she replied around her food, ketchup at the corner of her mouth.

"And the Sufflanders are always keen to help, right?"

"Like the Three Musketeers," said a man.

"Except without the floppy hats," said his twin.

"Good," said Izzy, "because there's a possibly life-or-death situation and I really need your help."

# 45

Carmella Mountjoy stepped imperiously across the lawns towards Penny. Penny glanced at her and then down at the dark where her phone had gone and where she had definitely — absolutely definitely — glimpsed the legs of a body in the well.

Carmella had called up to the house, her tone very much that of a country lady who had caught one of the village oiks scrumping in her orchard.

Frank Mountjoy, Jacqui Bildeston and Fliss Starling emerged in a snaking group from the house. Fliss held a cup of coffee in her hands. After a day and a night of celebration, it appeared the group had yet to prepare themselves for the new day. Susan, the housemaid or servant or whatever socially acceptable term rich people used these days, appeared from round the side of the house, sleeves rolled up as though caught in the middle of a cleaning chore. Monty ran a complex figure of eight around the arrivals.

"Look what I caught sneaking around in the garden!" Carmella declared.

"Penny?" said Fliss.

"The dressmaker?" said Jacqui.

"Doesn't she know Sunday is a day of rest?" snorted Frank.

Penny struggled for words and found herself saying, "I found your clothes line prop."

"What?" said Carmella.

Penny looked to Susan, who was frowning.

"It's down the well," said Penny and then, to Fliss, "I think you might need to sit down."

"What is it?" said Fliss, more impatient than curious.

"I've a good mind to call the police," said Frank.

"Yes, well…" said Penny and then, at her use of the word 'well', closed her eyes briefly. She took a deep breath. "I'm sorry, but I think I can see Will's body at the bottom of the well."

Fliss produced an incredulous laugh. Frank's scowl only deepened.

"It's true. I'm sorry. I'm really sorry."

Fliss put her hand out to place her cup on a table that simply wasn't there, then let it drop to the ground and scuttled forward in her wide hemmed trousers to the edge of the well.

"Be careful," called Jacqui.

"Please," said Penny. "I dropped my phone in trying to look but…"

"I'll call the police," said Frank, but Penny could tell it was more threat than helpful suggestion. "I will! I will!"

Fliss's knees buckled, but Penny and Carmella managed to catch her between them and guided her to one of the metal chairs.

"This is insane," said Carmella.

"It can't be," said Fliss.

"I think he's been down there some time. For days, at least."

Frank's lips popped in an explosive bark of derision. "We know he's been in town. We might not have seen him..."

Penny nodded and stepped carefully away from a shaken Fliss, leaving her in the care of Carmella.

"Yes. We all thought he was in town. His car was parked early on Friday, before anyone got up."

"I saw him!" snapped Carmella. "Out here. Morning coffee. Looking for hares in the field."

Penny gave it some thought. "Yes. Quite possibly. And then he was gone. And the car was parked in town and his wallet was found in the Crown and..." Penny turned around and pointed. "Izzy found his coat and hat on the scarecrow over there."

"What?" said Fliss, and now stunned alarm became something much more fearful and serious.

Penny shrugged helplessly. "All of which pointed to the fact that someone wanted us all to think Will was somewhere far from here because he was in fact..." She gestured at the well.

There was a blast of twelve-note Dixie airhorn and a roar of engine and, in a spray of gravel, a tall white Land Rover rounded the corner of the house and came skidding to a halt on the grass, removing a layer of turf in the process.

A door opened and Izzy tumbled out and came running down to them.

"Stop!" she shouted in her best cop voice. "Nobody do nothing!"

Penny stared at her. "That was quite an entrance."

"You alright?" asked Izzy. "No one tried to kill you or nothing?"

"Er, no." She gestured backwards. "Um, Will Starling's body is at the bottom of the well."

Izzy blinked and then went over and looked down into the darkness. Penny could see her mouth curling around some words.

"Don't say it," said Penny.

"Say it?"

"Just don't say it."

Izzy nodded and then said, very, very quietly, "Well, well, well."

Penny sighed.

"This is all simply too much for a Sunday morning," said Carmella.

"I think you should go," said Jacqui.

"Oh, too late for all that," said Izzy, waving her phone. "I've already called the police."

"Police? Why?" said Frank and then added, "I mean I said I would anyway but..."

Izzy put her hands on her hips. "Because we know who killed Derek."

"Do we?" asked Penny.

"The collective 'we'," replied Izzy. "Like, between us, one of us knows." She turned to address the unhappy residents.

"We thought Will had killed him."

"Didn't he?" said Penny.

"Preposterous," Fliss whispered.

"We thought it was some sort of jealousy. Maybe because of what had happened between you and Derek."

"Me and Derek?" said Fliss.

"And we thought maybe he'd discovered that Caroline was in fact Derek's daughter, not his."

Utter indignation managed to overwrite some of the shock on Fliss's face. "Me and Derek? I wouldn't even... ugh!"

"Unknown sources led us in that direction," said Izzy, looking pointedly at Carmella. Carmella deliberately angled her head away.

"We knew Derek was an unpleasant man at times," said Penny.

"Called me a chunky saucepot, he did," added Izzy. "And we knew he'd had something of a fracas with Jacqui the night before he died. And we thought that was purely him trying it on with her. But there were a couple of things Derek said when he drove me back to the shop that have stuck in my mind." She stepped back and pointed at the well. "You see, Will had money problems."

Penny looked apologetically to Fliss. "We noticed. He was a generous man but it was clear things were not okay financially. He was even selling his beloved Bentley."

"Exactly," said Izzy. "And several of you had commented that he'd only just managed to get it running properly recently. Derek even told me on that car journey that something was amiss under the bonnet. I thought he was talking about your friendships. Maybe he was. But then along came William Shatner."

"Shatner?" said Carmella. "The *Star Trek* man?"

Izzy nodded. "I mentioned that the mask from the old *Halloween* horror films was actually just a William Shatner mask painted another colour. And Derek seemed to find that more interesting than he really should have done. But of course he wasn't really thinking about William Shatner at all."

"Wasn't he?" said Penny.

"No. That's why he was suddenly full of questions for Jacqui at dinner. Questions about Monty's old red Bentley, the one that's a heap of junk in the shed. You see, I never stopped to wonder why Derek had died in the garage."

"He loved his car," said Jacqui. "He was... cleaning it or something."

"It was more than that," said Izzy. "He'd discovered something. I saw the fresh paint on Will's car earlier. It had to be patched up from where Derek had scraped the paint off earlier. You see, Derek had realised that Will had managed to fix his own car by stealing parts from Monty's old car. Both Bentleys of the same era with many interchangeable parts, I suppose. Not a great crime in itself, perhaps, but he had cannibalised Monty's car to fix his own, to solve his money problems. Derek discovered the truth perhaps only that very morning, and maybe Will came down by chance. Monty was barking and woke him."

By Penny's feet, Monty yipped.

Izzy shrugged. "They met. Derek made his accusations. Will perhaps tried to plead with him. Maybe there were the beginnings of an argument and there was a spanner nearby and…" Izzy sighed. "A spur of the moment thing. Manslaughter rather than murder, certainly. Will, frightened I'm sure, went back to bed and pretended nothing had happened. It was only by pure stupid luck that Frank thought he'd seen someone suspicious in the field."

"I did," said Frank.

"Scarecrow," said Izzy.

Penny turned to Izzy. "I thought you said Will didn't do it."

"Oh, he did," replied Izzy. "Right man. Wrong motive."

Penny let that all settle in.

"But Will," said Frank, stepping forward.

Penny understood. "If it wasn't for the line prop and the business with the car and the clothes, we might have thought that was an accident or even suicide. Will didn't mean to kill Derek, not initially. He was a loving and generous man. Too generous, perhaps." She stepped away from the well, contemplating it. "Another spur of the moment killing? Perhaps. Carmella, you did see Will taking coffee out here on Friday morning."

"I did!" she insisted.

"Possibly near the well. You see, it's now clear Derek wasn't the only one who had discovered that Will had dismembered Monty's car to fix his own debts. There was an argument here. Maybe Will simply tripped and fell." She gestured helplessly. "Maybe he managed to cling on to the side. I don't know. Did you use the line prop to push him in? Or did you use it to force him down when he got stuck halfway?"

It took some of them several seconds to realise that Penny was addressing this to Jacqui Bildeston.

"Me?" said Jacqui. She didn't strike Penny as a convincing liar.

Penny nodded sadly. "You, Jacqui, were the one Derek had shared his suspicions with at dinner the night before. You thought he was just being annoying and sticking his nose in, and then he died and perhaps his words suddenly resonated with you. Williams Shatner? Paint? The car?"

"Maybe you even went to look at the bits of your husband's car, to check," added Izzy.

"Maybe you didn't mean to kill Will, Jacqui," said Penny. "Not at first."

"This is all preposterous!" said Carmella. "You're upsetting everyone!"

"Maybe," agreed Penny.

There were flashing blue lights at the gate to Saxtead Grange. Monica had stepped out of her Land Rover to wave the police cars in.

"I remember our chat in the kitchen, Jacqui," said Izzy. "Death comes suddenly, you said. One moment you're then and then..." She gestured at the well. "Darkness takes you. And you said everyone gets their just desserts in the end. There *was* something like justice in what you did."

"We have photos of the Bentley being parked in the town," said Penny. "They're not great but I bet the police can do some clever computerised picture reconstruction thing and see who it really was in that cap and jacket. A cap and jacket that you, Jacqui, left on the scarecrow as you walked back here."

"And which you recognised when we were chatting in the kitchen," said Izzy. "You did offer to get rid of it. It was evidence after all."

Jacqui's face was pale and bloodless and quite still.

"I trusted Will," she said quietly. "I gave him my Monty's legacy and he decided to profit from it instead of giving me one thing to remember my husband by." She shot glances at each of the people around her. "It's not fair. I loved Monty and we should have had years together. We could all have stayed good friends. We could have stayed true. Happy. But so little of what could happen does happen."

She turned to meet the police officers approaching across the lawn.

## 46

Together, Penny and Izzy (and Monty) went to Miller Fields sheltered accommodation to find that the fete and open day was drawing to a close. The last cakes had been bought from the cake table, many of the stalls had packed away and there was only a scattering of prizes left at the tombola.

"Ah, someone won our rabbit toy," Penny noted.

"Rabbit toy?" asked Izzy.

"The one we made *especially* for the tombola," Penny said heavily.

"It was all moderately successful," said Nanna Lem, never one to heap high praise on anything unless it was truly deserved.

Glenmore was sweeping spent tickets into a box to be thrown away.

"I can finish up here," he said and so the cousins helped their grandma back to her room.

"Weren't you limping on your other leg last week?" said Izzy as they got her through the door.

"Er, was I?" said Nanna Lem. "Well, it comes and goes. I end up favouring one leg too much and then that puts strain on it and..." She dropped back into the sofa with a cushiony 'oof'. "Are we having a cup of tea, then?"

Izzy was onto it straight away.

"And how was the car show weekend?" Nanna Lem asked.

"Eventful," said Penny.

"I sold a ton of parasols!" Izzy called through.

"Do we do parasols?" said Lem.

"We do now!"

"We gained a dog," said Penny, gesturing to Monty.

"I was wondering..." said Lem.

"His owner was murdered and then, when we tried to take him back, the owner of the house they'd been staying at was also murdered and a guest was arrested for the crime."

"It all sounds very eventful."

"And I just solved another mystery, I think," said Penny.

"Oh?"

She picked up the purple felt hat on the arm of the sofa. "Izzy made this for you."

"Did she?" said Nanna Lem in a wobbly voice.

"Oh, knock off the doddery old lady act. You know she did."

"Maybe."

"I did see you on Saturday night. You were out dancing. Was that with Glenmore?"

"I don't think that can be right..." Nanna Lem tried.

Penny swung her finger back to point at the mantelpiece. "Then why is there a tiny Swing Dance Third Place trophy up there, hmmm?"

Nanna Lem pulled an embarrassed expression. She'd been caught out.

"Has Nanna Lem been secretly off dancing whilst pretending to have a poorly leg?" said Izzy, coming out of the kitchen.

"She has," said Penny.

"Does she belong to some sort of underground secret swing dance club where the first rule is you don't talk about swing dance club?"

"Less likely," said Penny.

"Fine," said Nanna Lem. "My leg's better, alright? It's been better for weeks. I'm sorry. I don't like lying to you girls but..." She sighed.

"But what?" said Penny.

Nanna Lem wrung her hands together. "I love Cozy Craft, I really do. That shop has been my life for decades but when I was forced to take a break because of my leg, I... I found I enjoyed having all the free time. I might be seventy-nine but there's still so much for me to do. Yes, the dancing. And I'm on the indoor bowls team. And there's the Thursday crafting group. I..." She reached out and took Penny's hands. "I do know you've got your own life to get back to in London, and I do know I'm holding you back. I just wanted to enjoy my little holiday a bit longer."

Penny felt Nanna Lem's hands in hers, the warmth of her small and still agile fingers.

"I think it's called retirement, Nanna Lem."

"Maybe, but I can't make you stay and it's not fair to leave Izzy to run the shop by herself."

Penny looked back at Izzy. "We do make a decent team," she said. "But I still have rooms I rent in London."

"I know," replied Nanna Lem.

Penny gave the older woman a penetrating look. "And you have no idea how much they cost me every single month. You daft woman, you. If you wanted me to stay on permanently, move myself down here, then you should have said."

"But it's not London."

"That's very true. Fresh air, green fields. The pavements not crowded with people rushing places with no time for you whatsoever. Here. I've got my own space."

Monty licked the side of her hand.

"And we've got a dog too now, apparently."

"Then you'll stay?" said Nanna Lem, not quite believing it.

"I'll be phoning my old landlord first thing in the morning, and I'll go collect my things next weekend."

"Oh, this is wonderful news. Time to break out the Battenburg cake. Izzy, I believe there's one at the back of the top cupboard."

Izzy paused on her way back to the kitchen. "Of course, one of the reasons Penny might be keen to stay is that there's a little shimmer of romance in the air."

Nanna Lem gave Penny a mischievous look. "Have you got a boyfriend?"

"No, not a boyfriend," said Penny. "Not yet."

"Oh. A suitor? A beau? A gentleman friend?"

"Just one gentleman friend, Nanna?" said Izzy with amused condescension. "You're not thinking big enough. Our Penny doesn't do things by halves."

Nanna Lem frowned. Izzy held up two fingers and made very expressive eyes. "Two," she mouthed.

Nanna Lem hooted with laughter.

# ABOUT THE AUTHOR

Millie Ravensworth writes the Cozy Craft Mystery series of books. Her love of murder mysteries and passion for dressmaking made her want to write books full of quirky characters and unbelievable murders.

Millie lives in central England where children and pets are something of a distraction from the serious business of writing, although dog walking is always a good time to plot the next book.

# ALSO BY MILLIE RAVENSWORTH

## The Sequined Cape Murders

Cozy Craft Mysteries can be read in any order. A funny whodunnit series, full of charming characters and mysteries that will keep you guessing to the very end.

Things are going great for Penny Slipper. Running a sewing shop in the middle of the English countryside is like a dream come true and she's got her colourful cousin Izzy and her corgi, Monty, to keep her entertained.

Her grandma's eightieth birthday is coming up soon and Penny and Izzy are busier than ever, making fancy dress costumes for the party guests.

However, Penny's dream life is thrown into chaos when a murdered woman is found in the bathroom of her cosy flat above the shop. With the doors and the windows all locked, no one can understand how this mystery corpse got there.

But things take a further sinister turn when a local shopkeeper is also killed. There's a murderer on the loose and no one is safe!

Can Penny and Izzy uncover the answers and unmask the criminal in their midst?

If your ideal book features mystery, friendship, cute romance, even cuter animals, crafting and a big slice of birthday cake then this is the book for you.

The Sequined Cape Murders

**The Swan Dress Murders**

Cozy Craft Mysteries can be read in any order. A funny whodunnit series, full of charming characters and mysteries that will keep you guessing to the very end.

A wedding is a cause for celebration. Not only do dressmakers Penny and Izzy get an invite to the big day but they have an unusual dress commission to complete for one of the guests.

It seems Penny's only problem is deciding which potential boyfriend to take as her plus-one guest — practical handyman Aubrey or cultured fabric expert Oscar.

But bigger problems arise when the maker of the wedding cake is found dead in the grounds of the stately home where the wedding is to take place.

And when another key individual in the wedding plans is also murdered, it seems like someone has deadly plans to prevent this marriage.

Can Penny and Izzy unravel the mystery and solve this crime before the big day is fatally ruined?

If your ideal book features mystery, friendship, cute romance, crafting and a charming rural setting then this is the book for you.

The Swan Dress Murders

Printed in Great Britain
by Amazon

25053213R00142